Buttermilk Hill

RUTH WHITE

SCHOLASTIC INC.

New York Toronto London Auckland Sydney
Mexico City New Delhi Hong Kong Buenos Aires

Thanks to Nora Baskin and Ginny Grant for their original poems created for this story.

The excerpt from "Any Day Now," words and music by Bob Hillard and Burt F. Bacharach, copyright © 1962 (renewed 1990) and assigned to Better Half Music and New Hidden Valley Music Co.; this arrangement copyright © 1993 by Better Half Music and New Hidden Valley Music Co., is used by permission. All rights reserved. International copyright secured

The excerpt from "Cry of the Wild Goose" by Terry Gilkyson, copyright © 1949 by Terry Gilkyson, published by Unichappell Music, Inc.

The excerpt from "Dreams" from *The Collected Poems of Langston Hughes* by Langston Hughes, copyright © 1994 by The Estate of Langston Hughes, is used by permission of Alfred A. Knopf, a division of Random House, Inc.

ISBN 0-439-85343-5

12 11 10 9 8 7   7 8 9 10 11/0

Printed in the U.S.A.   40

First Scholastic printing, January 2006

Designed by Robbin Gourley

For Margaret Ferguson, editor and friend,
and for Kay,
Lindy, Susanna, and Francie

Hold fast to dreams
For if dreams die
Life is a broken-winged bird
That cannot fly.

—Langston Hughes

Buttermilk Hill

1

Grandma Berry was not your typical grandma, with gray hair and specs perched on a pudgy nose—not at all. True, she had a few laugh lines around her eyes, and her hands were wrinkled up some. But she put a brown rinse on her hair to cover the gray, and she wore bright-colored polyester pantsuits with matching scarves around her neck to keep her appearance modern.

One Saturday night Grandma bent over to kiss me good night and said, "Piper, did I ever tell you that my first baby was born on my eighteenth birthday?"

I kissed her cheek. "And that was my daddy, right?"

I was spending the night with Lindy, and Grandma was tucking us in. Lindy was Grandma's youngest daughter, and my daddy's youngest sister, which made her my aunt, even though we were both ten.

Lindy and I had identical eyes—Grandma called them Berry blue—and the same freckles and blond hair. Folks in our little town of Buttermilk Hill, North Carolina, often made comments like "Ain't they cute together?" or "Them two could pass for twins."

We had cut our teeth together, learned the same nursery rhymes and fairy tales, sat side by side in school and church. We had celebrated holidays and family birthdays and anniversaries, worked in the garden and fished together, shared clothes, meals, and beds—all through sunshine and storms.

So of course I knew my daddy was born on Grandma's eighteenth birthday. I couldn't count the times I had heard this story, but it was a ritual Lindy and I never grew tired of—the song of the past.

There were many verses to the song, and this night we would hear one of our favorites. It seemed to us like it all happened ages and ages ago, to somebody else, in another lifetime, in another world.

"That means you were just twenty when Aunt JoAnn came along?" I said, yawning and snuggling under the sheets beside Lindy.

"That's right," Grandma came back, "and twenty-two when your Aunt Kay was born."

"Well, gosh, Grandma," I said, "you musta been old when Lindy came along."

Grandma laughed. "Old? I wish I was that old again! I was forty, and by that time my first baby—your daddy—was all grown up and married himself, to your mama."

"So you and Mama were expecting babies at the same time," I said.

"Yeah, your mama was expecting you while I was expecting Lindy."

"And that's how it happened that me and Piper got acquainted in the womb," Lindy finished the story.

"And I'm sure y'all found a way to carry on together with some kind of foolishness even then."

Lindy and I turned to each other and giggled.

Grandma raised the window just enough to let in the night air, along with the croaking of a million frogs. Then she sat on the bed again.

"Yeah, I'll have to say 1963 was a very big year for this family, with Piper being born in March, and Lindy in April."

"And why did you call me Lindy?" Lindy had to ask it, though she knew the answer perfectly well.

"For one thing, I liked the sound of it, and for another, it was the name of your great-grandmother on my side of the family. She was strong and good."

I didn't mention my own name. It was a sore spot with me that nobody thought of giving me a family name. No, my mama just had to name me after her favorite actress—Piper Laurie. Of course, she coulda called me Laurie instead of Piper—didn't I wish, not just because it was a nicer name, but also because Laurie and Lindy is more alliterative than Piper and Lindy. I had a good ear for alliteration.

"Time for lights out," Grandma said.

"One more minute!" Lindy begged. "Only one."

"Yeah, tell us about the Wild Girl!" I joined in the begging.

"Please, please, pretty please!" we said together.

Grandma sighed. "All right."

"It's a true story, ain't it, Mama?" Lindy reminded her to say it. We thought true stories were worlds better than made-up ones.

Grandma winked. "Oh, yes. Absolutely true." Then she began, nodding her head toward the open window. "There's a wild girl out there about y'all's size. When she was born, her mama stuck her out in the woods and left her, 'cause she was so ugly her family was ashamed of her.

"But the wild things took up for her and gave her food and shelter, and raised her. She's still out there, but she only comes out when it's nighttime. She's crafty at hiding. She learned it from the critters.

"Nobody knows where she lives, but folks believe it's somewhere close to one of the frog ponds. In fact, they say she's become part frog. Her face looks thadda way, you know? It's smushed up like a frog's.

"Anyhow, at night she tiptoes around under folks' windows and looks at them while they're sleeping, and tries to get into their dreams."

"Trailers, too?" I interrupted.

"'Specially trailers," Grandma whispered real spooky-like. "She loves trailers 'cause she can see into them easier than houses. They're closer to the ground."

I shivered and turned my face toward the hill behind Grandma's house. It was there that I actually lived in a trailer with my mama and daddy.

"For food, she eats roots and berries and whatever people

throw out," she went on. "For clothes, she rubs herself thick all over with mud from the frog pond, then she sticks leaves to herself so that when the mud dries she has a leaf dress sticking to her.

"And in the wintertime she steals people's stuff right off the clothesline. Mrs. Kindley swears that's what happened to a blanket she had hung out to air. She even saw little footprints leading into the woods behind her house over there."

Sometimes it was Mrs. Grundy or Mrs. Kluttz who had something swiped by the Wild Girl. I figured Grandma couldn't remember exactly who it was.

Grandma switched off the light as she left the room, and Lindy and I pulled the sheets up under our chins. Our heads were on the same pillow, our faces turned toward the open window. As the spring air caressed our cheeks, and our eyes slowly closed, we let the mythical Wild Girl come into our dreams.

2

The next morning, which was Easter Sunday, found us worshipping with the congregation of the First Lutheran Church of Buttermilk Hill, with all the Berrys and other townspeople. The church was packed that day, which was usual for Easter.

Mama and Grandma were singing in the choir, along with Mrs. Fisher, the Cheeps, the Sizemores, Mrs. Kindley, Mr. Kluttz, Mrs. Ridenhour, and other friends and neighbors.

Lindy and I were sitting near the back beside Mr. and Mrs. Early Mack, an elderly couple. Aunt JoAnn, Aunt Kay, and their husbands took up the rest of the pew.

Daddy and Papa Berry, along with Dr. Fisher and Mr. Driggs, were playing usher that day. When the preaching started, they sat on a bench in the vestibule.

Reverend Rivers was hitting the high point of his sermon when Mr. Mack, on my left, went to sleep and began to snore. Lindy and I, having been bored into oblivion, now came alive and started giggling. Funny things are always funnier in a place where you are supposed to be serious.

It was obvious that the people behind us also had the silly giggles. You could hear them stifling laughter in their gloves or handkerchiefs.

When Mrs. Mack finally poked her husband with her elbow, he woke up with a jerk, which shook the whole pew, and that made everybody laugh harder.

Mr. Mack's face turned red all the way to the top of his bald head and the tips of his floppy ears, and he stared straight ahead at Reverend Rivers, acting like he was hanging on to every word.

Things settled down a bit, and Lindy and I started playing a finger game between us that we had invented for long sermons. Sometimes our fingers got tangled up in the gossamer fabrics of our pretty Easter dresses.

I say *gossamer* because it was a word I had lately added to my list of favorite words. According to the dictionary, *gossamer* meant light and delicate, like a film of cobwebs floating in the air in calm, clear weather. To me, it seemed like a good word for describing the story of my life to that point—gossamer dresses, gossamer wings, gossamer dreams.

Soon Mr. Mack was asleep and snoring again. This time Lindy and I merely glanced at each other and smiled. Not long after, the snoring stopped, but it was obvious that Mr. Mack was still asleep. Everything would have been fine then if he had stayed in an upright position, but oh, no, he had to start falling over, and where was he falling to? Right toward me, and there was nowhere to scoot to, because the pew was full.

I stole a glance at Mrs. Mack, hoping she would notice and

poke him again, but she was staring out the open window beside her, at that gossamer day. I could see that she was totally lost in a reverie—another of my favorite words.

As Mr. Mack continued to fall, I moved as close to Lindy as I could. To me, this was not funny anymore, but the people behind us were hysterical, and a scene was being created right there in front of God and everybody.

Finally Mr. Mack's weight shoved me against Lindy. She, in turn, was pushed against Aunt Kay on her other side, who fell against her husband, Tim, who fell against Aunt JoAnn, who fell against her husband, Jake, who nearly fell out into the center aisle.

I peeped sideways at Mr. Mack and saw that his head was dangling at a funny angle, and his tongue was partially hanging from his mouth. At that same moment, Mama, up there in the choir beside Grandma, grabbed everybody's attention by leaping out of her seat.

This was definitely peculiar behavior for the middle of preaching. That's why all eyes followed her down the aisle, the big sleeves of her choir robe billowing, so that she appeared to be flying.

And where was she flying to? Right to me, where I was desperately trying to scoot out from under Mr. Mack's weight. Mama quickly stepped over Mrs. Mack, and that poor woman was so startled she bolted right out of her seat into the aisle beside her.

Only then did Reverend Rivers, who was annoyed, pause in his sermon. He did not like to be interrupted.

Looking into Mr. Mack's face, Mama lifted his head between her two hands, then, using his big ears as handles, she pulled him up off of me, as best she could. But he did not wake up!

"Dr. Fisher!" Mama called frantically, and she didn't have to call again. Dr. Fisher was there.

"Son of a gun, Mack looks dead!" somebody sputtered.

And so he did. And so he was.

That's when I started shrieking, and broke up what was left of the service. As Lindy and I scrambled out of the pew, we tromped on everybody's feet. We didn't miss a one. Then we ran out into the spring air, with Mama not far behind.

I didn't know it right then, but later, much later, I could look back and see that was the day the gossamer began to unravel—that Easter Sunday morning of 1973, when an old bald-headed man fell over and died on me.

3

There were six other trailers besides ours in the trailer park on the hill behind Grandma's house. In summer our park was covered with thick daisies, as was most of our town. The white flowers with their yellow centers reminded you of milk with golden flecks of butter in it. That's how our town got its name: Buttermilk Hill.

Daddy always promised we would have a real house someday with a brick chimney and all, but this trailer was the only home I had ever known.

From the front door of our trailer there was a well-worn path that led straight down to the back door of the house on Mill Street where Lindy lived with Grandma and Papa Berry.

That afternoon Daddy, Lindy, and I dragged our fishing gear out from under the trailer and went to the pond behind the trailer park.

When Lindy and I were in the first grade, Daddy had given

each one of us our own cane pole. He showed us how to put crickets on the hook, how to pull in our catch, and how to unhook the fish and place them on a stringer. We had all fished together at least once a week ever since.

We took our places on the bank of the pond and tossed our lines into the water. The dark, thick woods beyond the pond whispered and shivered in the cool breeze, but the sun was bright, and the grass was so green it almost hurt your eyes.

Lindy and I had cried about Mr. Mack until the tears had dried up. Now we were more than ready to forget that awful church scene and focus on something else.

Daddy, however, had other ideas. It looked to me like he saw an opportunity to talk to us about life and death and stuff like that.

"You know everybody has to die," was his opening.

"But not like that!" I said promptly. "Not falling over on top of somebody in church."

"And scaring the wits out of people," Lindy added.

Daddy smiled. "I don't reckon old Mr. Mack had much control over that. Do y'all think he did?"

We didn't respond.

"Given his druthers, I imagine he'd be like most of us, he'd druther die in his own bed in his sleep."

"Yeah, that's what I'm gonna do," Lindy said.

I didn't say anything, but I was thinking I'd druther not die at all, thank you very much.

"You might as well get used to it," he went on. "People die. It's a part of life."

I looked over at Daddy, who was tossing in his line for another try. I'll have to say he was right good-looking. He had the Berry blue eyes and dark, thick hair, which was crew-cut that spring. He was kinda short, but muscular and solid. After church he had put on blue jeans and sneakers. At thirty-one, he coulda passed for somebody's kid.

Then a chilling thought came to me: Daddy would die someday. Mama, too. And Grandma and Papa would probably go first!

"Yeah," Daddy said, "there are two things you have to learn as you grow up: you can't count on anybody to live forever, and you can't depend on anything to stay the same."

I didn't like hearing that, and I was afraid of what else Daddy might say, so I tried to think of something to change the subject with. Then Lindy did it for me.

"I got one!" she cried out.

I watched the sunlight glinting on the slippery golden scales of a fat bream as Lindy pulled him in. I smiled, thinking here was one thing that stayed the same: Lindy catching the first fish.

It was a relief to find something to smile about.

4

A few nights later, I had not been asleep for very long when I came awake suddenly. My bedroom was at one end of the trailer, while Mama and Daddy's was at the other. The living room and kitchen were in the middle, separated by a bar with three stools.

In the living room we had a television set on top of a bookcase, an easy chair, and a couch with a small coffee table in front of it. Mama and Daddy were sitting in there when I woke up, but they were not watching television. They were quarreling.

I ran my hand over the quilt Grandma had made for me, as I often did, trying to identify the pieces in the dark.

Here was the corduroy patch from a shirt Daddy wore in high school, and here was the flannel one from my baby blanket. Beside that was a cotton patch from the dress Mama was wearing the day Daddy introduced her to Grandma and Papa, then a silk patch from Grandma's wedding dress.

I loved this feeling of being warmly covered with treasured moments from the past.

As I fingered the patches, I listened to the night sounds and tried to pick out the voice of one frog that sometimes talked to me. He was louder than the others, and once I identified him, his "Rr . . . iibb . . . tt" changed to "Pi . . . ii . . . per."

I whispered, "Yeah, I'm listening, Old Croaker, what you want?"

"Pi . . . per, Pi . . . per grew out of her di . . . a . . . per."

He liked making up rhymes for me.

"Pi . . . per Ber . . . ry, always in a hur . . . ry."

Some of his words didn't rhyme too good, but they took my mind off the thing that was going on in the next room.

It seemed to me like Mama and Daddy had always been hollering at each other about one thing or another, but lately it was worse, lots worse. Me and Old Croaker tried to shut out the words, but we couldn't do it.

"I want more than this," Mama was saying.

"What more do you think there is, wife?"

"There's got to be more than housecleaning and laundry, cooking and taking care of Piper, churchgoing and . . . and PTA!" Mama spit out each word like it put a bad taste in her mouth. "You wouldn't be able to stand my life for one day, Denver Berry, you know that?"

There was a pause before Daddy suggested, "You could work for Papa at the Tarheel."

Mama laughed. "No, thank you, not interested."

"Just what are you interested in?" Daddy wanted to know.

"Well, it's not waiting on tables at a truck stop for tips. The

14

Tarheel was your parents' dream, Denver. Now it's their whole life—but not mine. I wish that's all it would take to make me happy."

"I'll tell you what would make me happy," Daddy said. "I want to have me a son and raise him up here in Buttermilk Hill, and live a simple life. That's all I want, and it's all you should want, too."

"We have nothing to offer another child!" Mama's voice was angry. "We're still living in a trailer, for crying out loud!"

"We won't always live in a trailer," Daddy said.

"But right now we do!" Mama went on. "And having another child would not be fair to anybody!"

"I'll tell you what's not fair," Daddy said. "That I've got only one kid and it's not a boy!"

It changed position in bed and counted the tree silhouettes against the night sky.

"I want to finish college. That would be enough." Mama's voice was pleading then. "Just give me those two years, Denver! Then maybe I can find out if there really is more."

"Having children is what it's all about!" Daddy's voice was stern. "We're born, we grow up, we marry, we have children, we have grandchildren, we get old, we die! Then our children do the same. That's all there is, wife. That's *all* there is! What makes you think there's more?"

Mama let out a long, heavy sigh. "When I was in the high school marching band, there was one girl who was always on the left foot when everybody else was on the right. We laughed at her, but now I know how she must have felt."

Daddy didn't say anything, and I figured he was like me—

didn't understand what some spastic girl a hundred years ago had to do with anything.

"I was going to be a music teacher," Mama continued. Were there tears in her voice? "I was so hopeful then. I had so many dreams. Now I spend my days doing nothing I can feel passionate about, and wondering when did those dreams die."

"Dreams, my hind end!" Daddy hollered. "You have your head in the clouds. That's your trouble!"

"You are quick to point out what my trouble is!" Mama hollered right back. "But you dreamed once; then you threw it all away! And that's *your* trouble, Denver!"

"Yeah, I was a kid! I did dream. And where did it get me? It's a cop-out!"

"You had a wonderful dream!" Mama was screeching by then. "You coulda been a major leaguer! You had a chance most men would die for, and what did you do with it? You blew it!"

"You shut up!" The sound of Daddy's voice nearly brought me out of the bed. "Don't you *ever* bring that up again!"

About half a minute later the front door slammed, rattling the whole trailer, and I heard Daddy start his truck and drive away.

This was becoming a habit with him. He might be gone for two hours or two days. I knew he was just going to the Tarheel, where he worked for Papa and Grandma Berry. He had been working there ever since he was old enough to help out.

When he was gone overnight, he slept in a room they had there above the truck stop. But he always came back home. Then he and Mama would make up, and things would be normal again for a while.

After the sound of the pickup was gone, the night was silent, except for the frogs. A light breeze teased my white ruffled window curtain, and I couldn't help remembering for the thousandth time how Mr. Mack had died on me.

I shivered, settled back on my pillow, pulled the quilt over myself again, and looked out at the moon and stars shining over our small hill. It was like a picture you would see on a calendar, and somehow it didn't seem right to have such hard words echoing in my head with all that loveliness out there.

Then I heard talking, dishes clattering, radios and televisions, and other normal sounds of the trailer park as folks picked up their everyday lives again. I knew they had stopped with their routines to listen to Mama and Daddy's quarrel just like we did sometimes when interesting things were going on in the other trailers.

In the Sizemore trailer, where there were four children under ten, a baby started crying, and Mr. Sizemore hollered, "Woman, stick something in that young'un's mouth!"

These were familiar sounds, and strangely comforting to me. I finally drifted off to strains of music floating on the night air, from somebody's radio.

Any day now I will hear you say,
"Goodbye, my love,"
And you'll be on your way
then my wild beautiful bird,
you will have flown, oh
Any day now I'll be all alone,
whoa-oa-oa-oa-oa . . .

5

Attached to our kitchen was a screened-in porch that Daddy had added onto the trailer. It was nestled among some trees, so that even when the trailer was hot, the porch was cool and pleasant.

That's where me and Mama were early the next morning, sitting at a table, enjoying the view of the pond, as we ate our cereal. Daddy had not come back home, and Mama hadn't even mentioned that he was gone.

"Last night, what did you mean when you said Daddy coulda been a major leaguer, but he blew it?" I asked Mama.

She let out a long sigh and moved a strand of brown hair away from her eyes.

"Well, Piper, your daddy had an offer to join the St. Louis Cardinals when he was eighteen years old, but he didn't take it."

I dropped my spoon. "The St. Louis Cardinals!"

"That's right," Mama said calmly. "The problem was that

the new players had to start with the farm team somewhere far off, and there was no guarantee that he would make the big team, so he decided not to go."

"And how come I'm just hearing about it?" I yelled, then answered my own question sarcastically, "Oh, I know, it's because *I'm only a girl!*"

Mama reached out and covered my hand with hers.

"He's not disappointed in you, Piper. He's disappointed in himself. He wants to have a son in addition to you, not instead of you."

"You mean somebody who can play baseball and make up for what he didn't do?" I said.

Mama went back to her cereal.

"Well, I've been living here for ten years, for crying out loud," I said. "And nobody bothers to tell me about the St. Louis Cardinals?"

"It hurts him to have the subject brought up," Mama said. "So don't ask him about it. It's the biggest regret of his life."

I watched her eyes as she gazed out at the pond thoughtfully. The first thing a person would notice about my mama was her size. She was a little bitty thing. In fact, her first name was Tiny. Foolish names run in our family, I reckon.

I could remember when my daddy used to say, "My wife's five feet tall, wears a size-five dress, size-five ring, size-five shoe, and she's five times better than I deserve!"

But he had not said that in a long time.

"You didn't know Daddy when he turned down the Cardinals, did you?" I asked, although I knew the answer.

"No; if I had, I would have *made* him take that offer. He might have flunked out, but then again he might have made it. Now he'll never know, and that eats at him—what might have been."

"When did you meet him?" I said, though I knew that, too. It was another one of my favorite verses to the song of the past.

Mama smiled at me. "You know."

"Tell me anyhow."

"Well, Daddy and I were students at Mountain Retreat College, and I asked him to the Sadie Hawkins Day Dance, and—"

"And he said he would go with you if he didn't get a better offer," I interrupted, chuckling.

Mama smiled. "Yeah, but he had a twinkle in his eye when he said it, and after that we thought we couldn't live without each other. Then at the end of the term we both quit college and got married."

Mama paused and closed her eyes like she was trying to remember something.

"Do you think he's coming back home?" I said.

"Doesn't he always?" she said, sighing.

I repeated everything to Lindy. Just like me, she didn't know about the St. Louis Cardinals.

"We could've had a major league baseball player in the family," she said with awe in her voice.

Then I told her what Daddy had said about wanting a boy. That made Lindy so mad I was almost sorry I had mentioned it.

"How could my own brother say such a mean thing? Even if he felt like that, didn't he care that you might hear him?"

But five minutes later she had changed her mind.

"You know, Piper, I've thought it over," she said. "And I don't think we should let it bother us. Maybe he really didn't mean it that way. I think he loves you a whole lot, and I agree with your mama that he was simply saying he wants a boy in addition to you, not instead of you."

Well, okay, that was Mama's and Lindy's opinion. Maybe it was true, but I couldn't help feeling hurt by his words.

It turned out Mama was right *and* she was wrong. Daddy did come back, but only to get his stuff a little at a time. He still came to the pond to fish with me and Lindy on Sundays, and I could see him any time I wanted to at the Tarheel, but he never spent another night in the trailer. Instead, he took up living alone in the room above the truck stop.

I had known for a long while that our family had a crack in it, but now I knew in my heart it was all-the-way broke.

6

"*Let's go for a ride,*" Mama said to me one day after school when Daddy had been gone for about a month.

We climbed into our puke-green Volkswagen, which I had named June Bug, and Mama drove us out of Buttermilk Hill into the countryside.

"Where we goin' to?" I asked her.

"Preposition Avenue," she answered.

I didn't know where that was at.

We rode in silence for a few miles. Then Mama cleared her throat and opened the conversation.

"You know Mr. Ridenhour, don't you?"

"Course I do."

It was a dumb question. Didn't I know everybody in Buttermilk Hill?

"You know he's a lawyer?"

"Yeah, so what?"

"Well, I went to see him about your daddy leaving. About us living apart. I asked for his help."

"Can he make Daddy come home?"

"No, he can't do that."

"Then how can he help?"

"He helped me draw up legal papers."

"What for?"

"So that everything's spelled out and made legal."

"Legal? That makes no sense, Mama. How can Daddy just up and leave you and me? Why would you want to make that legal?"

Mama answered in a calm, even voice. "Mr. Ridenhour knows about these things. He decides how much Daddy has to pay for your support, how often he can visit you, and—"

"Visit me!" I sputtered. "Daddies don't visit!"

"Your daddy and I will have joint custody of you," Mama explained. "He can see you any time he wants to, as he always has. But you will live with me."

"Then why go running to some old lawyer?" I asked.

"He recommended I get separation papers," Mama said, still calm. "Which I did. He said if your daddy and I live apart for one year, we can get an easy divorce."

There it was: that word nobody had yet spoken in my presence. It was a very big, ugly word—DIVORCE.

I had nothing to say.

"I want you to understand, Piper," Mama said.

In my head I was screaming, "No! No! I will never, never understand." But I said nothing out loud.

"We simply married too young, your daddy and I. We should

have finished school. But it's not too late. I can still go back to college. Your daddy didn't want me to do it, but it's something I have to do. You know, Piper, you have to follow your dreams."

She was really saying that *she* had to follow *her* dreams. It didn't matter what I wanted or what Daddy wanted.

"It'll be all right, Piper," Mama said as she reached over and patted my leg.

I shrank away from her.

"Your daddy and I both still love you. You know that will never change."

"Sure is funny how you show it!" I said hotly. "Daddy up and leaves us without so much as a kiss-my-grits, and then you go running to a lawyer as quick as you can to get a div . . ."

But that ugly word would not come out of my mouth.

We drove a long way out into the country. Mama did most of the talking, while I silently watched the farmland and the sky roll by. She told me how nice it would be when she became a music teacher. We would go on living in the trailer while she was in school, but then we could have a real house, maybe out here in the country. Wouldn't I like that? And we could travel together. Every summer we would go to a different place. Wouldn't that be fun?

At last Mama turned June Bug onto a dirt road leading to an old brown farmhouse way back off the blacktop.

"I know you're upset," she said, "but I have a surprise for you. It'll make you feel better."

She parked in front of the farmhouse and turned off the engine.

You could see tobacco growing in a field behind the house,

and the porch was so rickety I wondered how it could hold up that big old woman who stood there leaning against a post.

I didn't have much time to wonder because suddenly two giant golden dogs with flopping tongues and ears, along with seven little roly-poly carbon copies, came tumbling around the side of the house.

I got out of June Bug and fell down on my knees with the puppies. I was immediately covered with sloppy kisses, puppy breath, and happy tails.

Mama started talking to the woman, who was drooling brown spit. Her cheek was all pooched out, so I figured she was chewing tobacco.

"How much?" I heard Mama say.

Were we really going to buy one of these sweet, fat puppies? Did we have the money? Lindy and I had wanted a dog for always, and come to think of it, so had Mama, but Daddy wouldn't hear of it. Grandma and Papa wouldn't either.

Mama came over to where I was, and dropped to her knees with me. "Which one do you want?"

"Oh, Mama! We can have one?"

"Yes," she said happily. "Choose one."

It was nearabout the hardest thing I had ever done in all my ten years of life, picking just one puppy. But there was a spunky one who kept climbing all over me, licking me in the face and nibbling on my ears and fingers. It was like she was saying, "Pick me! Pick me!"

"You pest!" I cooed to the puppy, as I lifted her against my cheek. "You pesty li'l ole booger!"

"Is that the one?" Mama said.

"Yeah," I said. "She picked me."

"You can share her with Lindy," Mama said. "But she'll have to stay with us, because I know Papa won't have a dog in the house."

"You're our pretty Booger," I said to the puppy. "Piper and Lindy's Booger."

Then I kissed her right in the face. After I'd watched that old woman chew tobacco, it didn't seem like an unsanitary thing to do.

On Sunday afternoon Daddy was already at the pond when Lindy and I came tripping down the slope with our fat puppy tumbling happily along behind. Daddy dropped his fishing gear and propped his hands on his hips, watching us.

Lindy and I took our usual positions, with Daddy between us, but he was still in his exasperated pose, eyeing Booger.

"What's the meaning of this?" he finally managed to say.

"Whadda you mean?" I said innocently, and tossed in my line.

Booger started to run to Daddy, but I grabbed her just in time. She liked to be friendly to everybody.

"You know exactly what I mean!" Daddy said. "That dog there! Where'd he come from?"

"He's a her," I said, "and she came from Preposition Avenue."

"And whose dog is it now?" Daddy wanted to know.

"She's ours," I said. "Mine and Lindy's. Ain't she cute, Daddy?"

Daddy didn't answer, but frowned and turned away from me. Angrily he threw his line into the water, like he was trying to whip somebody with it.

After a while he said, "Did your mama go out and pay good money for that dog?"

"I reckon she did," I said.

"Does it stay in the trailer with y'all?"

"Yeah, she does. She sleeps with me."

Daddy shuddered with disgust, and said, "I have never lived in a house with an animal. They're nasty."

I could have said, "Then it's a good thing you don't live here anymore, ain't it?" but I would never say such a smart-aleck thing to Daddy.

"Do you know how big that dog is gonna get?" he went on crossly.

"Yeah, I know. She's a golden retriever. She'll get up to seventy or eighty pounds."

"Your mama has a lot of nerve complaining about the amount of child support I'm supposed to pay," he grumbled. "She says it's not enough money to live on. Then she goes out and buys this monster that's bound to eat y'all out of house and home. I wonder if she understands a thing about priorities."

"Understands what?"

"Priorities. Just ask her that."

So that night as Mama was tucking me and Booger into bed, I asked her, "Mama, what's priorities?"

"You and your words," Mama said as she smiled down at me and smoothed the hair away from my forehead.

"Do you know what it means, Mama?"

"Priorities? It's a list of things, ranked in order of importance. Why do you ask?"

"Daddy said to ask you if you understand priorities."

All the tenderness left Mama's face. "What were you talking about when he said that?" Her voice was icy.

"Booger. He said you fuss about not having enough money to live on, then you go out and buy a monster dog to eat us out of house and home."

"You can tell him yes!" she spit out. "Yes, I do understand priorities. And now that he's gone I can have the thing that's on the top of my list—joy!"

She left my room in a tizzy, slamming off the light switch as she went. I let out a long sigh and laid my cheek against Booger, who was snuggled in the crook of my arm, already asleep.

7

On a hot July morning, Mama and I were eating our breakfast on the screened porch when she said to me, "I've found a job as a waitress in Charlotte at an English pub called Mum's."

I had a sinking feeling. "What about me? Who's gonna look after me?"

"Grandma said you can stay with her and Lindy while I'm working."

"You mean I'll have to hang around at the Tarheel all the time!" I grumbled.

"Lindy and your grandma are not at the Tarheel all the time," Mama said.

Just most of the time, I was thinking. In fact, Lindy complained that Papa and Grandma never had time for her. In the past, she had often stayed with me and Mama. When Mama was out running her errands in June Bug, we had both hung out at the Tarheel.

"If you're gonna be a waitress, why don't you work for Papa and Grandma?" I asked.

"And see your daddy every day? No thanks."

I laid my spoon aside and sank to the floor to pet Booger.

"You know Grandma and Papa don't want to pay their waitresses a salary," Mama explained more calmly. "At Mum's I'll make two dollars an hour plus tips, and the tips are real good in a place where they sell beer."

A beer joint! I groaned, remembering all the bad things Reverend Rivers had to say about beer joints.

"I know it's not an ideal situation for you, but somehow I have to earn the money for college."

The very next morning we kissed Booger goodbye and left her alone on the screened porch with her chew toys, water, and food. Then Mama dropped me off at the front entrance of the Tarheel, and practically spun June Bug's tires out of the parking lot in her hurry to hit the highway. Mum's was on the edge of Charlotte, about twenty minutes away from Buttermilk Hill.

When I went inside the Tarheel, everybody was busy, so I walked to a booth near the kitchen where Lindy was already sitting. Grandma always let us have this spot, unless every table was needed. On those rare occasions, we had to sit on a bench in the kitchen until the place cleared out, which was no fun at all.

When we were younger, we had spent a lot of time coloring in our booth, playing games, or cutting out paper dolls. Later we took up drawing. Lindy was a super artist, while I was average. The thing she loved to draw most was houses. She would plan them inside and out, and decorate the rooms in bright colors.

The customers often dropped dimes on our table, which meant they wanted us to pick out something on the jukebox. We sang along soft to the songs we played.

When we grew weary of all that, we had library books to read. We both became good readers as we read aloud to each other.

The Tarheel had a delicious, comfy, homey smell. Grandma did all the cooking herself, or supervised it, and she was famous for her squash, green tomatoes, and okra—all fried, of course— also Brunswick stew, chicken and noodles, pork barbecue, sausage biscuits, eggs and grits, hash browns, you name it. Her cooking was as old-timey and southern as you could get.

Papa, Grandma, and Daddy worked long hard hours, doing everything from cleaning to busing tables. They got by with only two waitresses, Sally and Judith, who were old and gray-headed, and had been with the Tarheel for so long they seemed like a part of the family.

That day, after the midday rush, as Lindy and I sat there nibbling on grilled cheese sandwiches, Daddy managed to find time to sit down with us to eat his lunch. He brought with him a chicken salad sandwich and a big glass of iced tea.

These were my favorite moments at the truck stop—when one of the family joined us at our table. Daddy piddled around with small talk for a bit, then said to me, "So your mama's gone to work?"

"Yeah, she's gonna make two dollars an hour, plus tips," I boasted for her.

"Oh, is that right?" he said. "That's pretty good money for a waitress."

I didn't say anything.

"They serve beer in that place, don't they?" Daddy went on. I shrugged.

"Well, I want you to tell your mama something for me," Daddy said. "Tell her that she is setting a bad example for you, working in a place that serves beer."

After Daddy had finished his sandwich and gone back to work, Papa sat with us. His lunch was a bowl of Grandma's famous Brunswick stew.

Papa was an older version of Daddy—short and stocky, with Berry blue eyes, and a salt-and-pepper crew cut.

"How's my two best girls?" he asked as he slid into the booth.

Not only did Papa own the truck stop, he was also the mayor of Buttermilk Hill, and recently he had been responsible for erecting a sign by the highway near the Tarheel. On it was a picture of a cardinal, our state bird, and the words *Welcome to Buttermilk Hill, a Bird Sanctuary, Population 1600.*

"Exactly what is a bird sanctuary?" I asked Papa as he ate his lunch.

"It's a place where birds are safe, Little Bit," Papa said. "'Cause it's illegal to kill 'em within the town limits."

Sanctuary was immediately added to my list of favorite words. It was the sound of it that I liked, and its meaning—*a safe place.*

8

When Mama came to pick me up, she just pulled up near the window where Lindy and I were sitting. When I climbed into June Bug, she was practically bubbling.

"I made twelve dollars in tips my very first day!"

I sighed.

"What's the matter, Piper? Aren't you glad for me?"

"I'm tired," I grumbled. "It's hard to sit around the truck stop all day."

"Well, it's not for long," she said, trying to cheer me up.

"You mean you're gonna quit?" I asked hopefully.

"No, I mean school starts back in about five weeks, so you can spend most of the day in school. And next summer you and Lindy will be eleven years old."

"So?" I said crossly.

"I think you'll be old enough that you won't need somebody to look after you all the time. Y'all can spend part of the day at the trailer with Booger, if you want to, or go to

Grandma's house. Or just go back and forth. Won't that be fun?"

I looked out the car window at the neat white houses and the manicured lawns, and said in a mean voice, "Mama, Daddy said to tell you that you are setting a bad example for me."

I got no satisfaction in watching Mama's bubble burst.

"Oh, in what way?" she said coldly.

"By working in a place that sells beer."

"Well, you can tell your daddy," she snarled, "that maybe if he would lighten up and have a beer once in a while he wouldn't be so hard to live with!"

When we got home, Mama didn't even change clothes before she turned on the TV, kicked off her shoes, and flopped down in the easy chair. She was asleep in minutes.

I took Booger to the pond.

The next day I told Daddy what Mama had said. His eyes flashed anger, and he sent another message back to her. But I decided to forget what it was. Their hateful words made my heart ache. It was a mystery to me how two people who had once claimed to love each other enough to get married could hate each other so much now.

As time went by, I alternated from one day to the next on who was most to blame. First it was Daddy for being so headstrong. Why couldn't he let Mama do what she wanted to do? Would it kill him?

Then it was Mama for being so contrary. Of all the children I knew, nobody else's mama was a waitress, who wore short skirts and blue eye shadow even in the daytime, and served beer, and came home just give out and smelling like cigarette smoke and fried onions. If she would only act right, I thought, get off that left foot and back in step with everybody else, we'd all be happier.

Next thing I knew, she quit the church!

"You can go if you like, Piper," she told me. "The only reason I went in the first place was to please your daddy, and once I got started, I did love singing with the choir. But now I'm tired of that. There are other songs to sing."

So I had to go to church with Grandma, Papa, and Lindy while Mama stayed at home.

In the post office there were two mail slots. One read *Buttermilk Hill,* and the other read *Elsewhere,* which included all of those unknown, shadowy places outside the boundaries of our county.

Mama had always been referred to as "the Berry from Elsewhere" by the townspeople, and everybody knew who it was and what it meant. It meant that Denver Berry's wife was not a Buttermilk Hill native. This fact automatically placed her under a veil of suspicion.

Now, with her driving to Charlotte to work in a beer joint and quitting church, the tongues started wagging. Nobody was mean straight to her face or mine, but I heard things.

"I always did think she was backward."

"Just remember where she come from."

Or, a whisper and a giggle with the word "Hillbilly!"

Where Mama "come from" was a coal mining town in the southwest Virginia hills, but she didn't much like talking about it. She never returned there, because her mother had died, and her sister and two brothers had moved across the country. She talked to them on the phone sometimes, but they hardly ever saw each other.

Then one night Mama said to me, "Piper, I have decided to use my own name again—Tiny Lambert. It will be part of the divorce agreement."

Of all the bizarre things she had done, I thought this was the bizarrest. It meant me and my own mama would have different last names. I could imagine the good folks of Buttermilk Hill trying to comprehend such a thing.

"Why do you want to go and do something as peculiar as that?" I asked her.

"I have a perfectly good name of my own. Why should I go through life as Mrs. Denver Berry? Or worse yet—Tiny Berry!"

I had to admit she had a point there.

9

I can't remember exactly when I first got interested in rhymes, but I think it was when I started nursery school and Mama couldn't get me up of a morning. I didn't want to budge out of the little nest I had snuggled into, so she had to jump-start me. Instead of yelling at me, Mama would sit on the edge of my bed and read out loud.

In the beginning it was *A Fly Went By* and *Green Eggs and Ham*. I always loved anything that rhymed, and by the time she got to the last page, my eyes were wide open so that I could look at the pictures.

From Dr. Seuss, I had graduated to longer books with harder words, and after a while I started my list of favorite words in a special notebook Mama gave me as soon as I could write.

Gossamer . . . Reverie . . . Sanctuary.

In the fall of that same year when I was ten and Mr. Mack died on me in church, and Daddy left us, and Booger came to fill the empty place, and Mama went to work, a night came when there was a chill in the air, so that we had to go around closing all the windows.

Me and Booger snuggled together under Grandma's quilt, and I imagined the Wild Girl all wrapped up in Mrs. Kindley's blanket, shivering in her bed of moss and ferns. I dreamed that Old Croaker was packing his suitcase. The pond was getting too frigid for him, he said, and he was going to Elsewhere.

When I woke up the next morning, I found Mama perched on the side of my bed reading a poem to me just like she did when I was little.

> *October tiptoed in last night,*
> *While all the world was sleeping.*
> *I think she must wear rubber heels,*
> *So softly she came creeping.*
> *For when I opened wide my eyes,*
> *And saw the brown leaves fall,*
> *And felt the cool breeze on my cheek,*
> *I heard October call.*

I made her read it again, and again, until I had it memorized. I thought about it all day, and that night, in my little bedroom at the end of the trailer, I wrote my first poem.

Autumn
by Piper Berry (age 10)

> *A quieter friend has come to town*
> *to sew her gold on worn green gowns*

and slow the hurry of crowded streets
with cooler rhythms of autumn's beat.

A quieter friend has come this season
to bring a gift of rhyme and reason
and wash the worry of scurried minds
with falling leaves and sun more kind.

A quieter friend has come to town
to dress her earth in golden gowns
and hush the worry of troubled thoughts
with sweet fall breezes and harvest brought.

On Christmas morning Mama and I exchanged gifts and ate breakfast. Then I went to Grandma's house, where Grandma and Papa, Daddy, Lindy, and I opened more presents. I was to spend the day with them, while Mama drove to Charlotte and celebrated with some of her new friends from Mum's.

When Aunt JoAnn, Uncle Jake, Aunt Kay, and Uncle Tim arrived, there were even more presents to open. We played Christmas records and had a big dinner. Afterward we lay around the living room, groaning with misery from eating too much, while watching a football game on television.

Though this was very much like the past Christmases of my life, tears were just behind my eyelids all through the day. I couldn't get it off my mind that it was the first year I did not have Mama and Daddy together with me on this day, and I knew in my heart that Christmas would never be the same again.

I noticed that nobody mentioned Mama at all. It was like she didn't exist anymore. Only Lindy seemed to sense my mood, but she didn't say a word.

It was close to dark when Mama picked me up. That night I lay in bed, thinking about being a grownup woman someday, and having a little girl of my own. One thing I knew for sure— I would never divorce! I would not do that to my child. On second thought, I might not have children at all, or even get married.

I watched the moonbeams dancing on my beloved quilt. Then—was there a rustling beneath my window? Was the Wild Girl out there watching me? I tiptoed from bed and peeped out. Nothing stirred. The pond lay sleeping in the moonlight.

It seemed like a moment for making a wish. So with all my heart I wished that Mama and Daddy would get back together.

"And that's all I can do," I whispered to the moon. "I will give it to you now, and let it go."

A poem popped into my head right then, whole and complete, like a healthy newborn baby with all its fingers and toes. And I was comforted.

Mother Moon
by Piper Berry (age almost 11)

Mother Moon lays light soft on my quilted bed
pulling day's prickles from my sleepy head
and bending close by my ear she whispers:

This is, my child, the time now for
letting go of your mind's curious day
pushing your fears and your frets far away
I'll hold your good wishes safe in my beams
for I'm the mother of night's kind dreams.

10

On a cold January morning I woke up fever-
ish, with a sore throat, sniffles, chills, and aching joints.

"Hmm . . . mm," was all Mama said, as she felt my forehead.

A few minutes later I heard her on the phone, talking to her
boss at Mum's. "Can't come in today. Gotta take Piper to the
doctor and look after her. She's sick."

Sometimes when I was feeling puny, which was not often,
Mama could call Dr. Fisher up, and he would give her advice
right over the phone, or call in a prescription for us at Driggs'
Drugs. He might charge a dollar for that.

Other times I had to see the doctor face-to-face, and I knew
today would be one of those times. As Mama helped me dress,
I felt almost happy, in spite of being miserable. I would have
her to myself all day long, and I would also get to see Dr.
Fisher, one of my favorite people in the world. The doctor's office was on the first floor of his house on Apple Hill.

No matter how bad I felt, I always loved to look at the beautiful homes on Apple Hill, on the way to the doctor's office.

Mama's lawyer, Bruce Ridenhour, with his wife and boys, owned the biggest house on the hill. The pharmacist, Delbert Driggs, had the oldest. The Lucernes had a real fancy home up there, too, with their funeral parlor on the first floor. The Cheeps of Cheep Foods had a stone-and-cedar ranch.

In all, there were about twenty houses on the hill, but I thought none could compare with the one where Dr. Fisher lived with his beautiful wife and two teenage daughters. A two-story brick colonial, it had big round white columns and a circle driveway out front, a rose garden in back, wrought-iron lampposts, trellises with ivy, and other stuff like that all over the place.

Mrs. Fisher, the doctor's receptionist and main nurse, greeted us when we went in; then she took my temperature and weighed me, before ushering me and Mama into the doctor's office.

I sat down in a chair beside Dr. Fisher's desk. He tilted his head sideways and peeped out at me between his bifocals and big old bushy black eyebrows, while he fiddled around with his mustache and acted like he was puzzled.

"Who is this?" he said at last. "Do I know this young lady?"

"I'm Piper, Dr. Fisher." I had to talk through my stuffed-up nose. "You know, Piper Berry."

"No! No, it can't be!" he hollered. "But I delivered you only yesterday! I remember it well. You came out kicking and screaming, as wrinkled as a prune, and all red in the face. What happened to you?"

"Beans and taters," I said, just as he expected me to do. Those were the words of the doctor his own self when he was begging people to simplify their diets.

"Beans and taters! Beans and taters!" he preached to everybody who came in. "Meat has killed more people than cigarettes. It clogs up the arteries and causes heart disease. You will live longer without it."

Lindy was the only person I knew who actually listened to this particular bit of advice from Dr. Fisher. Except for fish, you couldn't pay Lindy to eat dead animals, but most of the good folks in Buttermilk Hill considered vegetarianism pretty dad-blamed radical.

"Of course!" he said with satisfaction, as he crossed his hands over his tummy. "You've been eating your beans and taters! And just look at what they've done for you! You're all grown up into a charming young lady overnight."

How could I help smiling and feeling better?

He glanced at my chart. "So you've got a bit of a temperature today?"

I nodded.

"And a runny nose and a sore throat, too?"

I nodded again.

The doctor listened to my chest and tapped on my knees, reminding me not to kick him in the nose.

"How old are you now?" he asked as he peeped around inside my ears.

"Almost eleven!" I answered proudly.

"Eleven years old? I'll declare!" Doc said, shaking his head. He couldn't get over it.

He opened a drawer in his desk, removed a book from it, and stuck it under my nose.

I read the title out loud. "*What Every Girl Should Know.* Is this about growing up?"

"Indeed it is," he said. "It's required reading, and next time you come here, Piper Berry, I want a book report!"

Then Dr. Fisher handed some sample pills and a prescription to Mama and gave her instructions. We drove directly to Driggs' Drugs at the corner of Apple and Mill streets. I stayed in June Bug with the heater running while Mama went in and got my medicine.

At home Mama followed the doctor's orders, helped me force the pills down with lots of orange juice, and tucked me into bed.

"You sleep now," she said gently. "I'll be here if you need me."

I snuggled under my quilt, feeling safe and warm. The medicine made me sleepy, but not in a normal way.

My muddled mind was trying to recall something about Dr. Fisher. A really tragic thing had happened to him. But what was it? I was almost too tired to remember. Did somebody leave him like my daddy left me and Mama? Yes, that was it, I thought, as I drifted away. I had heard the story. Long ago . . . long ago . . . before I was born . . . Dr. Fisher and his wife had lost a child.

11

"*I reckon it must be the first* Saturday of the month," Mrs. Grundy bellowed loud when she saw me and Lindy coming in the door.

It was spring again. We were eleven, and all the outside world was blooming pink and white and lavender blue.

"'Cause here comes the Berry gals to get a haircut," she went on, then turned back to her customer, who was leaving. "There you go. I'll see you next week."

"Goodbye now," Mrs. Sizemore said, and patted me on the head as she went out the door.

Mrs. Sizemore was my neighbor at the trailer park, the one with four children, but she still found time to clean up Mrs. Grundy's house once a week in exchange for having her hair fixed.

Mrs. Grundy called her shop the Curl Up and Dye. It was attached to one end of her house, across the street from the trailer park.

Mrs. Grundy was a chain smoker, and the odor permeated everything around her, including her rank breath, which you could smell when she was working on you.

I always looked forward to going to the Curl Up and Dye, not because I liked the smell a bit, nor because I liked sitting still long enough to get a haircut, but because I loved to hear the tales Mrs. Grundy was always telling.

In fact, she talked nonstop from the moment you climbed onto the adjustable chair to the moment you laid your two wadded-up dollars in her hand and went out the door.

You might get in an occasional sentence fragment while she was taking a puff, if you were quick. But that was okay with me and Lindy. We were anxious to hear the stories she had for us.

Lindy was the first to climb into the chair for her cut, as usual. While adjusting the chair for her, Mrs. Grundy lunged right into one of her tales. You never had to ask, and you never had to wait. That day it was about her mother. The grandchildren called her MeeMaw, so Mrs. Grundy did, too.

"MeeMaw is always putting castor oil on her moles and warts to make them come off," Mrs. Grundy said. "And I'll declare it works like a charm. But she had this real stubborn one. It was a great big wart on her index finger.

"She worked and worked on it for months, wrapping it up every night in gauze soaked in castor oil, and it got to the point it was just barely hanging there, but still there anyways."

Mrs. Grundy took a deep drag off her cigarette and coughed a deep rumbling cough. Fascinated, me and Lindy watched the smoke from her Virginia Slim curl out of her nose like wispy white worms.

Then she continued the story in her raspy smoker's voice. "MeeMaw told us, 'It'll take just a little longer, but soon this here wart is gonna fall right off like the one on my shoulder did.'

"So last Sunday evening my old man was gone as usual, to one of them everlasting Odd Fellows meetings; so me and my four young'uns went over to MeeMaw's house for a cookout.

"She mixed the meat and shaped out the hamburger patties with her hands, you know, like she always does, and we ate hamburgers till we thought we'd pop. I'll declare them was good burgers.

"So when we were done eatin', my baby Bubba looked at MeeMaw's hand, and said, 'Hey, MeeMaw, lookit, your wart's gone.'"

12

As summer approached, Mama and Grandma agreed that Lindy and I did not have to hang out at the truck stop all the time. We were allowed to stay in the trailer or at Grandma's house without supervision. And as long as we checked in every hour or so to let somebody know where we were, we could ride our bicycles or walk to places inside the town limits.

The day after school let out, the two of us, along with Booger, happily made our first non-official visit to the cemetery, which was smack dab in the middle of town. I say "non-official" because we had been to funerals there, but going to a graveyard for fun was a whole new experience. We picked the graveyard that day because we were tired of being pestered by little kids at the public playground. Here, except for the dead people, we were all alone.

With the past hanging like a heavy fog over the place, I

found that the cemetery, like the moonlight, brought out the poet in me. So the first thing I wanted to do was to wander among the graves, reading the tombstones, which we did.

"Some of these words are real sad," I commented, "but some are sweet."

"And some are both," Lindy said.

"Yeah, *bittersweet*," I said, thinking that was a word I wanted to add to my list. "Like this one here."

I read it out loud: " 'Dearest angel, Jesus loved you and took you home.' "

These words were chiseled on the headstone of a little girl who had been born in 1925, and died in 1928. Cherubs were perched on the rock, and the child smiled out at us from a yellowing photograph in a metal frame. Over the years the frame had started leaking around the edges, so that brown rust was running down the dimpled face.

We stared at the picture for a long time; then Lindy said, "I don't believe Jesus had anything to do with taking a three-year-old away from her family."

"Me neither," I agreed.

Another marker read:

JULIA LYND BURROWS
b 1919, d 1948

Many a flower
is born to blush unseen
and waste its sweetness
on the desert air

I imagined Julia Lynd Burrows one long-ago summer day, gliding through a field of wildflowers wearing a gossamer dress and a floppy, wide-brimmed straw hat.

"I wonder what she thought about when she lay down to sleep at night," I said dreamily.

"And I wonder did somebody miss her awfully when she was gone?" Lindy added softly.

"What kind of house did she live in?"

"Did her dreams come true?"

On the tombstone of Julius Cantor Fritz, b 1896, d 1962, were the words:

> We are such stuff
> as dreams are made on,
> and our little life
> is rounded with a sleep
>
> Wm. Shakespeare

I didn't know what it meant, but it gave me a chill.

In our bicycle baskets we had carried with us a picnic lunch and one of Grandma's old quilts, which we spread on the freshly mowed grass, under an oak tree near the street.

A sturdy iron fence separated us from the traffic, so we didn't have to worry about Booger. We sat down and looked around with satisfaction.

"I like it here," Lindy declared. "It's quiet and clean, with lots of trees."

Booger settled nearby to wait for scraps.

As we ate, we watched a caterpillar trying to cross the road without getting squashed. We were pulling for him, but he didn't make it . . . ugh. So we made up a fitting epitaph. I did most of the making up, but Lindy helped with her nods of approval or disapproval.

Crossing Roads
by Piper Berry (age 11)

Caterpillars
crossing roads
on their way
to become
butterflies

Some
go
on
to
fly

Others
go
in
to
butter.

Happily reciting our creation, we nibbled on peanut butter and jelly sandwiches and sipped cherry Kool-Aid. Then suddenly, among the summer sound of birds and katydids, the tree spoke.

"I gotta poem, too!"

We leapt from the ground with a squeal and looked up in the tree, and there, hanging off a limb, was Bucky Bark, a boy we knew from school. A year older than us, Bucky lived with his mother, Crissy, and they had no income whatsoever, except for a relief check from the government.

Bucky and Crissy Bark lived at the edge of the woods bordering Tacky Town, in a house that helped inspire the naming of the place. Of all the houses there, the Barks had the tackiest.

Though Tacky Town was the poorest neighborhood in our county, the people there were kind to Bucky and his mama, often helping them out by carrying them places in their dilapidated vehicles, or making minor repairs around their house.

The good people of Buttermilk Hill helped support the Tacky Town residents. From them came most of Bucky's clothes, and at Christmas the churches dumped bags full of toys and good things to eat on their doorsteps. The Lucernes had even given Bucky a perfectly good bicycle, which had belonged to their boy, Webster, a casualty of the Vietnam War.

"How long have you been there?" Lindy demanded to know.

Bucky laughed. "Does it matter?"

"What do you mean spying on people like that?" I said.

"Who's spying?" he said, and swung himself to the ground. "All I did was climb a tree, and you crept up underneath. Maybe you were spying on me!"

We were speechless.

Bucky grinned and said, "Wanna hear my poem?"

We still said nothing, but Bucky was not discouraged. He cleared his throat, folded his hands at his chest, and recited.

"Oooey Gooey was a worm,
A mighty worm was he.
He climbed upon the railroad track,
The train he did not see.
Oooey Gooey!"

Lindy and I busted out laughing.

Bucky grinned and said, "Now make one sentence with all four of these words: *defeat, deduct, defense, detail.*"

Of course we had no answer. *Nobody* did.

"De feet of de duck went under de fence before de tail!" Bucky said.

Again we laughed, and Lindy said, "Come on, Bucky. I know what you want—a sandwich and some Kool-Aid."

In high spirits, we all flopped down on the ground.

Booger, after sniffing around Bucky, was satisfied that he was not dangerous, and took up her begging stance again. I gave her part of a sandwich, and she got peanut butter stuck in the roof of her mouth.

She started throwing back her head and smacking her jaws, trying to get unglued, and we got the silly giggles.

When we finally settled down, Bucky said, "I had a dog once. His name was Liberace. You wanna know why I named him that?"

Lindy and I nodded.

"Because he was the pee—in—est!" Bucky squealed.

We laughed so hard then, we went rolling on the grass, holding our tummies. It was a delicious moment.

The dead people stayed dead, but watchful. The sun filtered down through the oak tree in speckles, and the sleepy town moved slow around us.

13

The next day we met Bucky again in the cemetery, this time on purpose.

"Can you think of a sentence that can be spelled the same backwards and forwards?" he asked, as the three of us rambled among the graves.

We couldn't.

"A famous one was said by Napoleon," he insisted, "when he was exiled to the island of Elba."

Who would know a thing like that?

"Able was I ere I saw Elba!" Bucky said triumphantly. "Try it. It spells the same backwards and forwards."

We came across two gravestones side by side that read *Cristopher and Rebecca Bark*. Bucky knelt down beside the graves and pulled a few weeds that had grown up between them.

"My grandparents," he explained. "Mama's mama and daddy. They died before I was born."

"Cristopher," I said. "So your mama was named after her daddy."

Bucky nodded.

"What's your whole name?" Lindy asked him.

"Buckroe Silver Bark!" he answered proudly.

"Did your mama name you after anybody?" I asked.

"No," he said quickly.

People said the identity of Bucky's father was Crissy's secret. I wanted to ask Bucky if he knew, but thought better of it. Folks said Crissy went a little off her rocker after Bucky's birth, and she never became Mrs. Anybody, or even Miss Bark. She was just Crissy, even to the kids. To be honest, we called her Crazy Crissy when Bucky wasn't around.

We soon learned that Bucky was in heaven when he was digging around in the dirt, making things grow. As the garden stuff came on, he brought baby tomatoes for us. They were locally called tommy toes, and he had raised them all by himself. People in Buttermilk Hill helped him with seedlings and gardening tools. With his vegetables, Bucky was able to win blue ribbons at the county fair, and at the same time he saved a lot of money for his mama at the grocery store.

When we talked about the future, Bucky had only one ambition: to be a farmer, and not just any old farmer. He would be the finest one who had ever used a hoe.

"I won't be one of them varmints who sit around dippin' snuff, acting like a dumb hick," he told us that day. "I'll go to college and find out about all the latest scientific methods, and I'll learn how to talk good and use my wit to charm the ladies and impress the men."

When I told him I was going to be a poet, he said, "Poet and don't know it, but your feet show it—they're Longfellows!"

Then he turned to Lindy. "And what are you going to be?"

"An architect," she promptly added.

"Good! Then you can remodel my house to look like Dr. Fisher's!" Bucky said.

"I didn't say a fairy godmother!" Lindy said, and we all laughed.

The day after that conversation, I was with Mama by the meat counter in Cheep Foods when I saw Bucky come in with Crazy Crissy. She looked so gosh-dern awful I knew Bucky had to be dying with embarrassment, so I turned away, pretending not to see them.

But I did see them for sure. I saw that Crissy was wearing men's overalls, cut off into shorts, with jagged uneven hems, and a white T-shirt underneath, turned dark with sweat. But the thing that made people do a double take in this hot weather was the combat boots reaching halfway up her legs. Also, her stringy red hair was crammed up under a cowboy hat, with half of it hanging down in her eyes. To top it all off, she was puffing a cigar, a habit I knew Bucky hated.

Peeping out from behind Mama, I saw Bucky trying to pretend he was not with Crazy Crissy. He meant to go his own way, but she grabbed him by the hair, of all things, and cried in a bullying voice, "Don't spend all day drooling over that candy counter, Bucky Bark, you heah me, boy?"

Everybody in the store heard her, and stared at her and Bucky. He jerked away from her, his face red as a tommy toe.

Then Bucky's mama came toward me and Mama. We were on the right at the rear of the store, and Bucky made a sharp left toward the candy counter at the front.

I could smell Crazy Crissy as she came up to the meat counter.

"I'll catch up with you," I said to Mama, and zigzagged through the store to the candy counter, where I found Bucky trying to make an important decision.

"Hey, Bucky," I said as cheerfully as possible.

He glanced over at me sideways, brushing back his hair, which needed cutting, as usual. He tried to grin, but it was plain to me he was still smarting with shame.

"What's up?" I said.

He held out his palm, showing me he had a quarter to blow, and I volunteered to help him pick something out.

Without knowing exactly what I was going to do before I did it, I reached over and patted Bucky on the back. It was an awkward move, but I had to let him know somehow that I was his friend, come what may. I didn't quite know what to do with my hands when I was through patting, so I folded my arms across my chest.

Bucky said nothing. He was like a statue. But nothing had to be said.

While we were standing there pretending that fire balls and Tootsie Rolls were the only things on our minds, we could hear a man greeting my Mama on the other side of the counter. I recognized the voice of a farmer who didn't get into town very often.

"Howdy there, Mrs. Berry. How're you doin' these days?" he said.

And Mama replied, "Fine, Mr. Redd, but my name is Tiny Lambert."

That's when I figured out the divorce was a done deal, and nobody had bothered to inform me, like it was none of my business, or something.

"Oh, beg pardon, miss," Mr. Redd went on. "I mistaken you for that Berry from Elsewhere . . . but now wait a minute, it is you! Don't you belong to Denver Berry?"

"I belong to no one." Mama pronounced each word clearly and distinctly. "You cannot own another person."

The man was just making conversation, I thought. He didn't mean anything. Nobody else's mother would pitch a fit over reg'lar conversation. Then there was silence.

When I turned my attention back to Bucky, I found his eyes were shining, and he had a peculiar smile on his face.

"Wow!" he said. "That was a groovy comeback!"

"Bucky, you're flirtin' with a hurtin'!" I snapped, thinking he was making fun of Mama.

"No, I mean it, Piper," he said with awe in his voice. "Honest, that was cool. I don't belong to nobody neither. I can't belong to her"—he nodded in the direction his mama had gone, though we could not see her—"'cause you can't own another person!"

14

"Oh, Piper, I love horses more than anybody!"

That was Lindy, who was sleeping over with me in the trailer, sniffling and wiping her eyes as we finished reading *Misty of Chincoteague* together for the third time.

"Me too!" I sniffed along with her.

It was the last weekend of the summer. The first time we had read *Misty* was last spring, in Mrs. Barrier's fifth-grade class, and it was all the invitation we needed to fall head over heels in love with every horse in the world. Since then we had read *National Velvet*, *My Friend Flicka*, and *Black Beauty*, then *Misty* again two more times.

Booger placed her chin on the side of the bed and looked at us sadly. She was imploring us to invite her to come lie between us. She had been rooted out of her usual spot because there was not room for all three of us in my bed.

"Don't worry, Booger," Lindy said. "We'll not forget you. We love horses, but we love dogs, too."

Taking Lindy's sweet tone as an invitation, Booger jumped up on the bed, curled herself between our feet, and sighed contentedly. She was already half-asleep. Lindy and I looked at each other and smiled, not having the heart to put her out of the bed.

"She feels left out down there on the floor," Lindy said.

I rubbed Booger's head, and she grunted. "Yeah, she's used to sleeping with me."

I turned off the lamp, and we arranged ourselves as best we could with eighty pounds of dog holding the covers down.

Lindy said, "Tomorrow let's ask Papa and Denver if maybe we can have just one horse for the two of us."

Several times we had already asked for horses. We were sure Aunt JoAnn and Uncle Jake would be delighted to let us house them at their farm out in the country, where they had a big old barn, and not a single animal using it.

But the whole horse idea had been vetoed by Daddy and Papa. Maybe they would reconsider if we asked for only one.

"All right," I agreed. "We'll try that."

Then both our heads turned automatically toward the window. I imagined the Wild Girl darting across the hill while Lindy and I slept and dreamed of horses.

We spent the next day with Bucky, and late in the afternoon the three of us bicycled to the Tarheel. Lindy and I chained our bikes behind the truck stop, where we usually left them overnight. Then we went inside and settled in our booth. There were about ten customers in the place, and they were locals.

"Y'all want anything?" Judith the waitress called to us from her stool by the cash register.

We shook our heads and waited for Daddy and Papa to emerge from the kitchen to take a break. They always did that just before the supper rush. After a while, here they came out together with cups of coffee, and we motioned for them to come sit with us, which they did.

Papa was also carrying a plate full of french fries.

"Here, boy, eat these taters!" he ordered, and shoved the plate under Bucky's nose. "We made too many, and I can't stand to see food go to waste, can you?"

Bucky's face lit up. We knew french fries were an uncommon treat for him, though the rest of us were tired of them.

"Gee, thanks!" he said, and made a dive for the ketchup and salt shaker.

So we sat there laughing and joking around while Bucky ate his fries, and Papa and Daddy drank their coffee.

After a while Lindy said, "Guess what, Papa? We have decided that we'll be happy with just one horse for the two of us. We'll share it!"

She beamed at Papa, certain that this bit of news would win him over.

"And we are positive that Aunt JoAnn will not object," I added, "not if it's just one horse."

Daddy and Papa smiled at each other. Their amusement was irritating.

Bucky wiped the ketchup off his face, pushed back his plate, and sat perfectly quiet, looking from one face to another.

"Oh, I'm sure JoAnn would love that!" Daddy said sarcastically.

"Right! I'll bet she can't hardly wait!" Papa added.

And they actually laughed!

At that moment Mama came inside the Tarheel to pick me up, which was unusual. For some reason she was early and I was not looking for her.

Daddy was the first to see her walking toward us, and he said in a loud voice, "Piper, tell your mama to get her head outa the clouds. It's catchin'!"

He laughed again. Mama's face went red as she reached us.

"Piper, tell your daddy it's better than anything you'll ever catch from him!" she shot back in a voice as loud as his.

With that, everybody in the place laughed, and it was Daddy's turn to have a red face. Mama grabbed my arm, jerked me to my feet, whirled fast on her heels, and headed for the door, yanking me along behind her. I felt Bucky's pitying eyes on me all the way out the door. I figured if anybody could relate to this embarrassment, it was him.

On the way home Mama was seething with anger.

"What was your daddy talking about?" she demanded to know.

"Horses," I said. "Lindy and I asked for just one horse to share, and he made fun of us!"

"Horses!" Mama practically spit at me.

"Yeah, horses!" I said. "We love horses, and nobody understands. Nobody!"

"You'll get over it!" she snapped.

"See! You don't understand either!" I wailed.

"I understand that an obsession with horses is typical for girls your age. It's a phase you're going through."

"Typical?" I screeched. *"A phase?"*

With a few words, she had reduced all my tender longings to ordinariness.

"And what about you and Daddy keeping secrets from me?" I asked. "Is that a phase y'all are going through?"

"What secrets?" she said, turning to eye me.

"My name is Tiny Lambert!" I said in a prissy, mocking voice. "I don't belong to nobody!"

Mama was silent.

"You've got your name back," I said. "So it's all settled, and nobody bothered to tell me. I've known it for weeks. Did you think I wouldn't find out?"

"I was going to tell you," Mama said, all of her anger gone, "at the right time."

We reached home. She shut off the motor and turned to face me.

"I'm sorry about what I said, Piper. I do understand your love of horses. I'm sorry you're not able to have one. I'm mad at your daddy, and I took it out on you. As for the divorce, it's not an easy thing . . ."

But I climbed out of June Bug before she could finish one sentence about that nasty word. I slammed the door of the car as hard as I could, went in the front door of the trailer, fetched Booger, and ran out the back way with her down to the pond before Mama was out of the car.

15

To our great surprise and delight, Daddy
and Papa talked things over, and decided to let me and Lindy
take riding lessons on Saturdays at a place out in the country
called Rentz's Harness Shop. They sold all kinds of neat horse
stuff there, like saddles, bridles, and blankets, or you could have
your horse shod, if you were lucky enough to own one.

Our teacher was a cute young fellow by the name of Jimmy,
and he started the lesson by introducing us to our horses, Taffy
and Greenleaf. We were so thrilled to actually be this close to a
real horse we got the jitters and couldn't stop giggling.

So Jimmy let us spend the first ten minutes just talking to
the horses, stroking them, and absorbing their special smell.

Then our lesson began with the boring stuff, about saddles
and bridles and bits. After that we spent some time just sitting
in the saddle while Jimmy led us around a field and taught us
basic commands. We listened to every word he said.

Back in the stable, we learned about caring for our animals after riding them, and the hour was up. We said goodbye to Jimmy, Taffy, and Greenleaf and met Grandma in the parking lot.

"Well, how'd it go?" she wanted to know.

But she could tell by our excited chatter, red faces, and shining eyes that riding lessons were sure to be the most fun we'd ever had. The following weekend we found to our disappointment that we would be riding another pair of horses.

When we asked to have Taffy and Greenleaf every time, Jimmy said to us, "It's not allowed. Part of the lesson is to learn the different temperaments of the different animals."

So he didn't understand us either, and once again we were right back to feeling that sad ache for a horse of our own.

On the Saturday before Thanksgiving, Lindy and I were at the Tarheel, fixing to eat lunch after our riding lesson. Daddy served me a fat juicy hot dog, smothered in Grandma's homemade chili and onions. Then he placed a big green salad in front of Lindy and sat down with us.

"I've got a job driving a truck," he announced with a grin on his face.

"Will you make lots of money?" I asked, then wrapped my mouth around the end of the hot dog. It was almost too much to cram in there.

"Five twenty-five an hour, double time on Sundays and holidays," he went on proudly.

"Then you can buy me a horse!" I said quickly.

"Yeah, a horse!" Lindy agreed, and Daddy laughed. He was in a good mood.

"I reckon you'd keep a horse in that trailer with your hound dawg?" he said to me.

I smiled, thinking I would if I could.

"But, Daddy, what about your job here at the Tarheel?" I said.

"Yeah, Papa's gonna miss your help," Lindy said.

"He understands," Daddy said. "He knows I need more money. He said he'll hire your mama to work in my place. Why don't you ask her about it tonight? Tell her at least she won't have to serve beer here."

"Okay," I said, thinking it would be real handy to have Mama working at the Tarheel instead of at Mum's.

"Something else I have to tell you," Daddy went on as he placed his arm across the top of the booth behind me. "I've met a nice lady, and I'd like you to meet her."

I felt a flash of anger. He meant he had a girlfriend!

"Who is she?" Lindy asked.

"Her name is Melba. She's from Kannapolis. She works there at Cannon Mills, you know, where they make the towels and sheets? She has twin boys, Lewis and Larry, and they are eleven years old, just like y'all."

So she had boys! Well, wadn't that a feather in her cap?

"I'm going over there to her place tomorrow evening for a cookout," Daddy went on. "She wants y'all to come, too, okay?"

"Sure," I said, feeling no enthusiasm whatsoever. "That'll be fun."

"I can't," Lindy said. "I promised Mama I'd help her deliver Thanksgiving baskets over at Tacky Town."

How lucky could you get?

When I asked Mama if she was interested in taking Daddy's job at the Tarheel, she gave me a flat no. Papa had already called her and asked, she said, and he didn't plan to pay her nearly as much as he paid Daddy.

"After all, I am only a woman," Mama said sarcastically. "Never mind that I would be doing the same work your daddy did. With tips at Mum's I can make more than what Papa is offering."

"But at the Tarheel, you wouldn't have to serve beer," I argued. "Daddy said to tell you that."

"Piper," she said with a laugh, "you can tell your daddy I'd rather serve poison than work at the Tarheel! There's nothing there for me."

I sighed. It would do no good to remind her that I was there much of the time.

16

On Sunday evening Daddy came for me in his pickup, and we drove to Kannapolis to the cookout with Melba and her boys. We rode through the countryside in silence for a piece.

"You're mighty quiet," Daddy said at last. "Ain't you happy about going out with your daddy tonight?"

I just shrugged.

"Whatsa matter?" Daddy tugged at the hair over my ear. It was a thing he used to do when I was a baby.

"It's just that I always hoped you and Mama would get back together," I said sadly. "But now I feel that's never going to happen."

"Well, honey, I tried," Daddy said sweetly. "Several times I attempted a reconciliation, but she wouldn't listen."

"Wonder why she wouldn't, Daddy?"

"Oh, Piper, you know your mama. She thinks she's missing out on something. But she's a daydreamer, and she's on a wild-goose chase!"

A wild-goose chase? I looked out at the rolling North Carolina landscape, and I could almost hear Mama singing that song about the wild goose.

> *My heart knows what the wild goose knows,*
> *And I must go where the wild goose goes.*

Melba was large, not exactly fat, but a fraction taller than Daddy, big-boned and jolly. It seemed like nothing would make her mad.

"Hello, you sweetheart," she welcomed me. "At last! I've been wanting to meet you for the longest, and your daddy was always saying, 'Sometime . . . sometime.' You know how he is?"

Yeah, I knew. And it made me wonder just how long this had been going on.

"And these are my ball players here." Melba pointed to Larry and Lewis, who were dressed in baseball uniforms that said *Kannapolis, N.C., Home of Cannon Mills,* on the back. They were sprawled in front of a television set, drinking Sundrop.

"Hey," they said together as they looked up at me, and immediately went back to their shoot-'em-up show.

"They're some boys," Daddy said proudly, like they were his very own. "You orta see Larry hit that ball. And pitch! Lordy mercy, Lewis is gonna make a pitcher, shore as the world. Major league material, both of 'em."

Well, whadda you know about that. Major leaguers.

And so it went. All evening I heard Daddy and Melba go

on about their boys, and coo to each other till I felt I might puke.

The hamburgers were greasy and reminded me of Mrs. Grundy's wart story. So I decided to tell it. The Devil made me do it.

I finished up the story just like Mrs. Grundy had done: "And then Bubba said, 'Lookit, MeeMaw, your wart's gone!'"

I glanced from one face to another, but they all stared at me like they were waiting for more.

"See?" I said with a grin. "She mixed up the hamburger with her hands."

Nobody laughed. Nobody even smiled.

"I'll declare," Melba said seriously. "Do you reckon that wart fell off in the hamburger meat?"

"Oooooo," Lewis said, scowling at me and shoving his plate all the way to the center of the table. "I can't eat now!"

"Oh, shush, Lewis," Melba said. "It's just a story. It didn't really happen, did it, Piper?"

"Yeah, it did," I said, just as serious as Melba. "Somebody ate that wart for supper."

"Make her shut up, Mama!" Larry hollered as he shoved his plate back, too.

I smiled sweetly at him.

"Piper, honey, you shouldn't talk about such things while we're eating," Daddy said.

"She don't know no better," Lewis said with a nasty smirk on his face. "Her mama's a hillbilly."

"Lewis!" Melba scolded. "That's not nice."

"Well, Denver calls her that."

So that was the game—them against me and Mama.

It was a relief to get back home.

"How'd it go?" Mama said brightly as I came in the door, but I didn't answer. I was surprised she was still up.

I went into my bedroom and slammed the door. I undressed quickly and climbed under my familiar quilt. Mama came into my room and sat down on the edge of the bed.

"Wanna talk about it?" she said, and I had a sneaking suspicion, call it a premonition, that Mama wanted to hear some dirt about Melba and her kids. It would give her some kind of giddy satisfaction.

"It was fine," I said. "I'm tired."

Which was true.

"Okay," she said with a sigh. "But if you want to talk—"

"Good night!" I interrupted her.

She bent over and kissed me, tucked me in, and left me alone. There were no sounds from the other trailers, so I figured it must be after midnight.

A cold autumn wind was whipping over the hill, and I pulled my quilt up close, running my hand over the section of curtain patches.

Here's the first pair of curtains ever to grace the Tarheel—red-and-white-checked, naturally. Here's the Dr. Seuss Mama had decorated this bedroom with when she was expecting me. And here's the curtains Grandma had hung in Daddy's dormitory room at Mountain Retreat College.

So once again I was comforted by the song of the past, and before sleeping I made up this poem:

Grandma's Quilt
by Piper Berry (age 11)

Grandma's quilt, snug and warm,
is my haven from winter's snowy storms
a keeper of sleep and of kind night tales
a shelter from summer's thundered gales.

Grandma's quilt was sewn from care
with each stitch meant to soothe night's mares.
Grandma's patterns seem to be
ways into the best of my dreams

And in the night when I fall deep,
with prayers and promises in thought to keep
Gram's soft quilt will hold my sleep
like coats of wool hold winter sheep.

17

I hardly ever saw Daddy after that. He was gone for days at a time, sometimes driving all night, but he was proud to be making $5.25 an hour, double time on Sundays and holidays. When he had a day off, he spent it with Melba and the future major leaguers.

I saw Mama every night, but she seemed distant. I could feel her slipping away, too, and I couldn't hold on.

The customers at Mum's were always giving Mama things for tips instead of money, which was nice of them, she said, but she needed the money more.

One customer who claimed to be a musician down and out on his luck gave Mama his guitar. She was thrilled over that old battered-up thing. She bought a book called *Teach Yourself Guitar* from a Charlotte music store, and she decided she would learn to play.

Mama spent hours plunk, plunk, plunkin' on her guitar, in the middle of the night, for crying out loud!

Sometimes she kept me awake, and I hollered at her. "Mama! I am trying to sleep!"

"Okay, hon, just one more song."

When spring came again and the windows were opened, the neighbors started hollering, "Shut that thang up for a while, would'ja?"

It was like throwing shoes at a yowling cat, but the next night she was right back at it again.

Plunk! Plunk! Plunk!

Then she let her hair grow out long and straight and parted it in the middle. She started wearing faded blue jeans, and sometimes she wore a bright headband across her forehead. Nobody else's mama looked like a flower child from the sixties!

When I finally saw Daddy again, Mama and I were coming out of Cheep Foods as he was going in. The two of them did not speak to each other, but Daddy hugged me.

Then he said loud enough for her to hear, "Piper, tell your mama she looks like a hippie!"

"Piper, tell your daddy he looks like a redneck!" she shot back, and kept on walking. I had to run to catch up with her.

"Who's the kid and who's the adult here?" I said sadly when I repeated it all to Lindy.

"You should let them know how much they embarrass you and hurt you," Lindy said angrily.

But I knew confronting them would only make matters worse because each one would start blaming the other.

When Mama found out how much money Daddy was making at his new job, she pitched a fit. Next thing she did was take him back to court to get more child support out of him.

That's how she managed to pull enough money together so that she could drop half of her hours at Mum's and enroll at the University of North Carolina at Charlotte. At Mountain Retreat College she had started working toward certification as a music teacher. Now she planned to continue toward that goal.

So at last Mama became a college student. She car-pooled with another student named Guy Webb, who lived down the road a piece from Buttermilk Hill. He came up Route 49 and swung by the trailer park to meet up with her.

One week Guy drove to UNCC, and the next week he left his Karmann Ghia parked in front of the trailer while Mama drove. Each Wednesday Mama had to take June Bug by herself, because that was the day she worked at Mum's for eight hours, then eight hours again on Saturday and four hours on Sunday.

When the school year ended, me and Booger hung out with Lindy and Bucky almost all the time. Mama was never at home, and when she did have some time off, she had to study. She often complained that college was hard for her. But I couldn't help thinking it wasn't half as hard for her as it was for me.

18

In late summer I got some important news from Daddy
and Melba. They were getting married in October, and they
wanted me and Lindy to take part in the ceremony. That's
how it came about that Melba put together my first homemade
dress, and I didn't quite know what to think of it, so I decided
to get Mama's opinion. Big mistake.

During a rare moment at home, we appraised the dress.
Mama helped me put it on, and I went around and around in
front of the mirror. Without saying anything at first, she stood
in my doorway with her chin in her hand. We both studied it,
imagined me in it at the wedding, and thought about all the
pictures that would be taken.

The dress was ankle-length and had long, puffy sleeves. That
was okay. But I wondered what Mama would think of the
bright yellow color with orange flowers in it. And the polyester
material. Would she smirk? Yeah, Mama was a smirker. I bet
she'd smirk.

"Well," she said at last, "it's serviceable, Piper."

"Whadda ya mean?" I said.

"I mean it'll never wear out. Maybe you can hang it over your window for a curtain when you've outgrown it."

She 'bout died laughing then at her own cuteness, but I was too aggravated for words. She just had to do that, didn't she? She just had to make fun because Melba had made it.

Lindy had to wear the same dress. She and Grandma both said they thought it was a "perfectly lovely dress," so I acted like I thought it was perfectly lovely myself.

The wedding was planned at the First Lutheran Church early in the afternoon. For me, the whole thing was just something I had to get through with a smile on my face, and I was relieved when it was over.

Afterward we went to Grandma and Papa's house for a celebration dinner with the two families. Melba's mama was dead, but her daddy and brother were there, along with Lewis and Larry. On Denver's side were Papa and Grandma, Aunt JoAnn and Uncle Jake, Aunt Kay and Uncle Tim, Lindy, and me.

Near the end of the meal all the guys left the table carrying pieces of wedding cake on dessert plates, and went to the family room, where they flopped down in front of the television set to watch the first game of the World Series.

The rest of us were still seated at the dining room table picking at our cake when Melba said, "Well, we won't see them again until the game's over. Let's do girl talk."

Girl talk? My eyes met Lindy's for just an instant. Then we both looked away quick. We didn't want to laugh at Melba on her wedding day.

"I want y'all to be the first to know, we're expecting a little'un in April!" Melba gushed.

Grinning from ear to ear, she waited for a reaction from us.

Grandma, Aunt JoAnn, and Aunt Kay all hugged her and congratulated her, then tried to think of something else to say. Lindy and I slurped our lemonade loud.

But Melba wasn't finished. She was full of surprises.

"Another thang," she went on. "Denver is gonna adopt the boys!"

"That's nice, Melba," was all Grandma said about that.

"Yeah, then y'all can have the same last name," Aunt JoAnn said. "All four—I mean five—of you."

"What about their real daddy?" Aunt Kay said. "Is it okay with him?"

"He don't care!" Melba grumbled. "He'll be glad not to have to pay child support anymore!"

That meant my daddy would be responsible for the twins' support. The girl talk was going bad. All the "girls" were just looking at each other with question marks in their eyes. Like me, they were probably wondering whatever had possessed Daddy. Had Melba bewitched him?

A commercial came on the television, and someone turned the volume way down, so you couldn't help hearing what was being said in there.

"Dad," we heard Larry say.

They were calling him Dad already? But of course.

"Yeah," Daddy answered him.

"Why didn't you take that offer from the St. Louis Cardinals?"

So Daddy had shared that bit of information with the twins? And he had never bothered to share it with me.

"I don't know," Daddy mumbled. "I reckon I didn't know any better."

"You won't never get another chance like that again in your whole life!" Lewis said triumphantly, like he was announcing an important revelation.

"Prob'ly not," Daddy said sadly, and at the table all of us looked away from each other. "But I was good, boys, real good," Daddy went on. "Always remember that. Like Marlon Brando said in that movie, 'I coulda been a contender.'"

I clenched my teeth together. Oh, sure, he coulda been a contender all right, but why think of that now? Here he was, thirty-three, with two wives and three and a half kids to take care of!

The celebration broke up after the ball game. Daddy and his new family left for Kannapolis, where they would live in Melba's house. It was raining real hard, so Papa drove me up the hill to the trailer. He kissed me on the cheek before I got out of his truck. That was so unlike Papa I had to wonder if he knew what was going on in my head.

"It's all gonna be okay," he said softly. "Just give it some time. You're still my Little Bit."

I had to smile. He hadn't called me that in a long time. I put my arms around him. A moment alone with Papa was a rare treat.

Inside the trailer I found Guy Webb and Mama sitting on the sofa together watching *The Jeffersons*. I hurried into my room before Mama could ask me any questions.

Booger was all curled up on my bed asleep. Had she been banned from the living room to make way for Guy Webb? Would I be next? Booger wagged her tail at me, and I lay down, pulled Grandma's quilt over me, hugged Booger close, and listened to the rain falling on the tin roof.

19

The following Friday night Mama had a date
with Guy Webb. They were going out to dinner at a fancy
restaurant. I had never seen her so excited.

I was in the kitchen fixing myself a sandwich, while she was
in her room getting dressed, when Guy knocked at the door.

"Put Booger out on the porch!" Mama hollered. "And tell
Guy I'll be ready in a minute!" And she closed her bedroom
door.

I laid my sandwich on the bar, thinking I would eat it later.
Then I shoved Booger out onto the back porch, and let Mama's
date in the front. He stood there with a bouquet of flowers in
his hand.

Guy Webb was right good-looking, in spite of the fact that
he was losing his hair. Mama had told me that he was actually
younger than her, and the balding was premature. He was tall
and slender, with nice brown eyes and a boyish face.

In the past, the two of us had done no more than nod at

each other in passing, so I figured this might be a good chance to get to know him.

"Hey there, come on in and sit down," I said as pleasantly as I knew how.

Without a word he came in and perched on the couch, clutching the flowers in his fist. The six-thirty news was going off, and Walter Cronkite was saying, "And that's the way it is, Friday, October 17, 1975."

I took a vase from under the sink and offered to place the flowers in water.

Guy handed the bouquet to me without a word, keeping his eyes on the TV screen, even though there was nothing on it now but a Dippity-Do commercial. I put the flowers in the vase with water and set it on the coffee table.

"So, Mr. Webb," I said politely, because in Buttermilk Hill every older person was Mr. or Mrs. unless they told you to call them something else. "How are you these days?"

And I sat down beside him.

"Fine," he muttered, without looking at me.

"What are you studying to be?" I opened the topic of conversation by showing an interest in him. I had learned that in social skills class.

But he looked at me like I was an alien and had spoken to him in a foreign tongue. "Beg pardon?"

"You go to college with Mama, don't you?"

He nodded.

"So what're you studying?"

"Education."

Education? I was puzzled.

"But which part of it?" I went on doggedly.

Guy Webb gave me an aggravated "Huh!" and looked at his watch. What a jerk! But I could take a hint. I went to the bar, sat down with my back to him, and ate my sandwich.

A few minutes later Mama came out of her bedroom in a cloud of perfume, all dressed up in a black cocktail dress, looking fit to kill.

"Piper honey, did you say hello to Guy?" she said in a kittenish voice I had never heard her use before.

"Yeah, we spoke," I mumbled.

"Well, couldn't you keep him company for one itty-bitty minute?"

One itty-bitty minute? I felt my face go hot with embarrassment for her. She sounded like a retarded Scarlett O'Hara. Next I expected her to say "Fiddle-dee-dee."

Before I could respond, Guy was standing up. "Let's go."

Mama was all smiles for him, making over the flowers like she'd never seen a daisy before in her life, with a ton of them growing right outside the door every summer.

A few minutes later they were leaving, and Mama remembered my existence again. "You'll go on down to Lindy's now, won't you?"

"Yeah, Mama, I'm on my way," I said.

And that was that. She was gone. I let Booger in and gave her the last two bites of my sandwich. I cleaned up my crumbs, put Booger back out on the porch, gave her fresh water and dog food, kissed her on the head, and apologized for leaving her.

Then I took the worn path down to Grandma and Papa's house, where I was to spend the night with Lindy.

As Lindy read aloud to me that night from *Stormy, Misty's Foal*, my eyes fell upon one of many framed pictures she kept on her nightstand. This one was of Mama and Daddy, taken shortly after they started dating at Mountain Retreat College. I picked up the picture and looked at it.

They were sitting on a rock in the woods, with speckles of sunshine filtering down through the branches upon their smiling faces. They both wore blue jeans and appeared to be about sixteen years old, though they had really been around twenty.

"I wonder if they ever think of those days," I said to Lindy.

She studied the picture, but said nothing.

Then I told her about Guy Webb, how rude he had been to me.

"Sounds like he hates kids," Lindy said.

"Just think, if Mama marries him, I won't have any escape at all. I'll have that little grouchy, boy-faced bald man on the one hand and mushy Melba and the terrible twosome on the other."

Lindy giggled. "You'll just have to come and live with me and Mama," she said.

"Yeah, I wish," I said.

It had been a long time since we had asked Grandma for a story at bedtime. Maybe it was because we had outgrown her stories, or maybe we had heard them all too many times.

But that night I felt like hearing a verse from the song of the past. So when Grandma came in to say good night, I said to her, "Tell me about the first time Daddy brought Mama home with him from college for the weekend."

"Oh, you don't want to hear that old story," Grandma protested. "We've worn it out."

I showed her the photo I was still holding in my hand. Silently, Grandma took it and gazed at it tenderly.

"So young," she mumbled.

"Please tell it," I begged.

So she told us the story, which I already knew by heart. Aunt JoAnn and Aunt Kay were teenagers, and the whole family had gone out to eat at the Captain's Galley Fish Camp and get acquainted with Denver's new girlfriend.

"And Mama was wearing that blue dress that's in the quilt now," I said.

"That's right," Grandma said. "And she looked very tiny and pretty."

When we had gone over the details again and again, Lindy said, "Tell us about the Wild Girl now."

We had not asked for that one in a long time either.

"The Wild Girl!" Grandma sputtered. "Here you are twelve years old. Haven't you outgrown that old story by now?"

We smiled up at her, knowing she was going to tell it, the same way she used to do those many nights when we were little.

But Grandma surprised us. "Do you know, when I was a girl, my mother told me that story?"

"When *you* were a girl?" I said. "But the Wild Girl's *our* age, Grandma!"

Grandma laughed.

"Oh, no, Piper, the Wild Girl is ageless. My mother heard about her from her mother—you know, the one Lindy is named after."

"Why'd you never tell us that before?" Lindy said.

"I don't really know. Why didn't I?" Grandma said quietly, like she was talking to herself. "Maybe I was remembering how disappointed I was when I found out she was not real."

"But she *is* real!" Lindy and I said together.

"When I was a teenager, I heard that she sprouted wings and learned to fly," Grandma said dreamily. "That's my favorite story about the Wild Girl."

She learned to fly? My eyes searched the darkness behind the window.

"Yeah, just like a bird," Grandma went on. "I heard she flies all over the country, but she always comes back home where she belongs."

All weekend I thought about Mama and Daddy and the days when they had first loved each other. By Monday I had created a poem that made me feel better.

Missing
by Piper Berry (age 12)

*What do we do
with the missing
that's left behind
after you've moved on?*

If we plant it
like a seed
in the ground
does it grow into an oak?

If we give it
to the river
then to the sea
is it lost as a treasure?

If we bury it
in the mountains
will it be turned
into amethyst or gold?

Or, if we send it
to the stars
does it become a bridge
to heaven . . . to your heart?

What do we do
with this missing
you
now that you've moved on?

20

Early the next spring Lindy and I gave up our horseback riding lessons at Rentz's Harness Shop.

"We have learned all that Jimmy has to teach us," Lindy explained to Bucky as, once again, we were sitting on a quilt, picnicking under a tree in the cemetery.

"And we still don't have a horse of our own, so what's the use in lessons?" I said.

Bucky nodded absently. He seemed to be in a place of his own that day.

"What's on your mind?" we had asked him more than once, but he'd answered, "Nothing."

Since Bucky never talked about his home, I sometimes felt he had no life away from us, like maybe he lived only in our minds, and appeared whenever we thought of him. So I was surprised when, after a while, he said, "Mama's been acting real weird."

"Weird how?" Lindy asked.

"She does some peculiar things," Bucky went on, and I could see worry in his eyes.

"Like what?" Lindy said.

"Well, she goes into the woods, and she comes out crying. She cries a lot."

"Your mama cries?" I said incredulously. I couldn't picture it.

"And why not?" Bucky snapped. "Doesn't everybody cry sometimes?"

"Yeah, but your mama—"

Lindy poked me with her elbow, and I shut up.

"As far back as I can remember, I've seen Mama going into the woods ever' once in a while, not often," Bucky went on, "and she came back home crying. But lately she does it every day. I followed her twice. I hid behind the trees and watched her. Both times she goes to this certain spot beside an old rotten log and kneels on the ground. It's almost like she's praying, but Mama is not a religious person."

"And she does that every day?" Lindy said.

"Now she does. It's weird, don't you think? Another thing, she has started writing something, and she hides it from me. I've never known her to write before. But she's busy with it every night when she thinks I'm asleep. When she's finished working on it, she locks it up in an old wooden box she's got. There's a padlock on it."

Lindy and I looked at each other with big eyes. Wow, a mystery!

Our sandwiches lay uneaten beside us, and Booger kept creeping closer and closer to them.

"And she takes some kind of foul tonic that she mixes up in the kitchen sink. It stinks something awful."

"What do you reckon is in it?" I said.

"I don't know what all she puts in it—molasses for one thing, and brown mustard for another."

Molasses and mustard? Yuck.

"Old folks sometimes have special remedies they learned long ago from other old folks," I said. "Maybe it's one of those."

"Yeah, I think that's what it is," Bucky agreed. "But my mama ain't old, Piper. She's about the same age as your mama."

I almost blurted out, "No way!" but I held my tongue. Crazy Crissy seemed *lots* older than Mama.

"She gets up in the wee hours of the morning and takes the stuff. That's what bothers me," Bucky went on.

"Then she must be sick," Lindy said. "Maybe she's in pain."

"Has she been to Dr. Fisher lately?" I said.

"We don't go to Dr. Fisher," Bucky said, which was news to me. I thought everybody went to Dr. Fisher.

"We don't go to the doctor much at all," Bucky went on, "but when we have to go, Marvin Johnson—you know, our neighbor—drives us over to see a doctor in Charlotte."

"How come?" I said.

"I don't know for sure," Bucky said. "I never understood it myself. Maybe Mama owed Dr. Fisher some money and he wouldn't treat her, or something like that."

That made no sense to me. I knew Dr. Fisher treated people who didn't have any money.

"Well, has she been to the Charlotte doctor lately?" Lindy asked.

"Not that I know of. Unless she went when I was in school, and she didn't tell me."

At that moment Booger pounced upon Lindy's sandwich, and gobbled it up so fast Bucky laughed for the first time that day.

"When I'm an old farmer, I'm gonna have me a dog like Booger," he said affectionately as he rubbed her on the head.

"When I'm a famous poet, I'm gonna write a poem called 'Booger' that will immortalize her."

"Immortalize? Well, lah-de-dah, don't we talk fancy?" Bucky teased. "A new word for your list?"

"My list is so long now I can't remember what's on it."

"And when you are an architect—" Bucky said to Lindy, but she interrupted him.

"When I am an architect and an interior decorator," Lindy said. "Yes, then I'll design and decorate your farmhouse and Piper's loft. Every poet needs a loft."

But that day my imagination didn't want to dwell on this picture of the three of us being all grown up with a place of our own, and maybe apart from each other. I didn't want to imagine not having Lindy, not having Bucky to talk to, to listen to, to be with. No, I had come to accept that Mama and Daddy would never get back together, and I had learned to like the present. I liked being this age and living in this time and place.

21

Daddy and Melba's baby was born on Lindy's thirteenth birthday, three days after the twins' thirteenth birthday. It was a girl, and they called her Laurie. Grandma said she would throw one big party for all of them every April.

Then there was Piper, born in March.

Papa, Grandma, Lindy, and I went together to the hospital.

Melba said she picked the name Laurie because it started with the same letter as Larry and Lewis. Then Lindy pointed out that her name started with an "L," too. So now it was Lindy, Lewis, Larry, and Laurie Berry. Very alliterative, I thought.

Then there was Piper.

Not only did Piper start with a "P," but Laurie was the name I had always wished was mine. It gave me the most peculiar feeling that I had been replaced.

While we were all standing there looking into the nursery window, Daddy said, "Lindy, now you have another niece, and, Piper, you have a half sister!"

Suddenly I was lonely for Mama, and I just wanted to get on back to the trailer, but I knew she was out with Guy Webb again. Suppose Mama married him and they had another little girl. Then where would I belong?

Mama didn't mind at all that Daddy had another family. In fact, she wished them happiness, and I think she meant it. But that was before Daddy and the new Mrs. Denver Berry bought a big house out in the country near Aunt JoAnn's farm.

Then Mama didn't wish them happiness anymore. She wished them leprosy.

When school let out at the end of May, Daddy and Melba called and said they wanted me to spend more time with them.

"We want you to feel like this is your house, too," Melba said generously.

My house, too? I was flattered, but also wary. I always felt left out when I was with them. Maybe I would be more comfortable if Lindy would go along, I thought. It would be like having somebody join my team instead of having to play alone against all of them.

So I asked if Lindy could come with me the first time, and everybody was agreeable. Happily Lindy and I packed for a weekend in the country.

The twins were proud to give us the grand tour. The new place was beautiful, and huge. Only five years old, this house had originally been built for a family with six children.

Upstairs there were four bedrooms. One was for Daddy and Melba, the boys pointed out to us, and the one beside it had been turned into a nursery for the new baby. The other two belonged to Larry and Lewis.

"Where are me and Piper gonna sleep?" Lindy asked the question I was thinking.

The twins shrugged without answering Lindy's question.

But Lindy didn't let up. When we went downstairs to the big breezy yellow kitchen, we found Melba warming up a bottle for the baby.

"Where are me and Piper gonna sleep?" She repeated her question to Melba.

Melba took the bottle from the stove and dripped a little of the milk on her forearm before answering, "Oh, don't worry, you don't have to sleep outside!"

And she laughed like she had said something really clever. Later, Lindy and I were in the family room when we overheard Melba in the kitchen, fussing at the twins in a low voice.

"I told you a hundred times, one of you will have to give up your room when she's here! So y'all decide!"

In the afternoon a hard rain came down, and Melba started making fudge while Lindy and I played Uno with Daddy, Larry, and Lewis at the kitchen table. Baby Laurie was asleep.

There was a huge window right beside the table that overlooked the rolling farmlands, and I kept staring out there, thinking how much Mama would love to have this house.

The green glistened in the rain, and you could see somebody's farm animals at a distance. I could write me a poem about this view, I was thinking. Something like . . . rooting piglets in the rain . . . wrapped, as if in cellophane . . . spotted cattle, white and black, caught in rain without a mac . . .

I was dreamily lost in my poem when Melba brought me back to the moment by saying, "Lindy, I know you eat mostly veggies, and we have plenty of them, but Piper, what do you like? What do you want for supper?"

"I want hot dogs!" Lewis said before I could answer.

"No, we had hot dogs last night," Larry said. "Let's have spaghetti tonight."

"I think it's time for steak," Daddy said. "We ain't had steak for a long time."

"Yeah, steak!" Larry and Lewis said together.

"I'll go to Cheeps' and pick up some T-bones," Daddy said. "And we'll fix 'em outside on the grill if it quits raining."

Lindy punched me under the table and our eyes met.

I like fish! I was screaming in my mind. *I like fish fried to a crusty golden finish the way Mama used to fry 'em for us when we were a family!*

I looked out at the wet green land again and tried to pick up the poem, but I had lost my train of thought. Lindy was watching me. I felt like crying, but I would never do that in front of Lewis and Larry, not in a million years.

So I swallowed hard.

We finished our Uno game in silence, and the twins went in the family room to watch television. Daddy kept on shuffling the cards absentmindedly. I watched Melba pour the thickened fudge onto a clean white plate.

"I like fish." I spoke up then, surprising even myself. "Lindy does, too."

"Oh . . . you do?" Melba said. "Fish? What kind?"

"Well, I like bream the best, fresh-caught, but we don't have any of them."

Daddy cleared his throat and changed positions heavily. I

was trying to remember the last time he had gone fishing with us. Maybe he was trying to remember, too.

"Hmmm," Melba said. "What do you like second best?"

"I like those baby catfish like they have at the Captain's Galley."

"Maybe we could go to the Captain's Galley tonight!" Lindy suggested. "All the fish you can eat for one low price of $3.95 each."

"Plus tax," I added.

"And french fries and coleslaw and iced tea," Lindy went on.

"And hush puppies!" I hollered, clapping my hands together.

Melba smiled. "We'll try to do that one of these weekends when it's not raining."

Daddy got up and put on his raincoat and galoshes.

"Come on, boys!" he hollered to Lewis and Larry. "Let's go buy some T-bones while the women toss up a salad and bake a few taters."

A big pain was creeping into my heart. Way back when I was his little girl, Daddy took me places with him. He sometimes carried me on his shoulders. He always wanted me with him.

But now, I thought with a sigh, I would have to push aside those thoughts. I wanted to finish my poem, and those ghosts from the past did not belong in it:

In the Rain
by Piper Berry (age 13)

Rooting piglets in the rain
wrapped as if in cellophane

shine a pinkish piggy sheen
piggy plump, and piggy clean!

Spotted cattle, white and black
caught in rain without a mac
wear socks of mud up to their knees
huddled under cattle trees.

Cozy sheep dressed all in wool
wade in rain through little pools
leading little lambs astray
lest the babes should float away.

Ponies wet in dampened coats
protected by their pasture moats
stand like regal kings and queens
ruling o'er their Kingdom-Green.

Soggy cats in wilted fur
relieved, it seems, of their purrs
washed ashore on front porch chairs
licking rain from un-sunned hair.

Cawing crows in tops of pines
dressed in black, dressed in shine
perched in trees like weather vanes
calling out, "Here come the rains!"

After supper, Melba announced that Larry would give up his bedroom for me and Lindy this time, and next time Lewis would give up his. Larry was not gracious about it. He slammed things around for half an hour.

"We want you to feel like this is your house, too!" Melba had said to me on the phone. Yeah, right! I would never have a spot to call my own in this house.

22

The next Friday evening Mama and I were eating tomato soup and grilled cheese sandwiches, and watching *Sanford and Son*, when the phone rang. Mama answered, grunted, and handed the phone to me. I could tell by her attitude who was calling.

Melba told me that Daddy would be out of town until late Saturday night, but if I wanted to come for the weekend anyway, she would pick me up. I was ready with a white lie.

First I sniffed and coughed. "Thanks, Melba, but I think I'm coming down with something, and I sure wouldn't want Laurie to catch it."

"Maybe next weekend," Melba agreed quick enough. "Your daddy will be here then."

I was relieved as I hung up the phone. I had a whole week to think up another excuse. I sat back down with my supper and tried not to notice Mama was smiling.

"Coming down with something, huh?" she needled me.

"Yeah." I found myself keeping up the lie because I couldn't stand that smirk on her face. "You can't be too careful with a baby."

Mama laughed out loud then.

"Piper, you can't fool me! You hate it there, don't you?"

Why did that give her so much pleasure?

"No!" I protested. "I like it. It's fun, really."

But Mama went on laughing. She could see right through me, and it was maddening.

I escaped to my room. Actually, I was looking forward to a wonderful weekend with Lindy and Bucky. The thought made me smile as I gazed out toward the pond, where the evening light was fading away.

These days Papa allowed us to talk on his CB radio in his pickup. It had become one of our favorite things to do together.

"It don't cost anything," he said to Grandma, when she had questioned him about it. "And they enjoy talking to the truckers."

"As long as you don't tell anybody who or where you are," Grandma had said to us. "And I mean it! You don't know what these truck drivers might be up to."

That was Grandma putting her foot down, which she didn't do very often, so we figured we better listen.

The very next day found the three of us sitting in Papa's truck, which was parked out behind the Tarheel.

"Breaker one-nine, this is Little Bit, you copy?"

We nearly always got a reply from a trucker going by on the highway.

"How's your mama?" Lindy asked Bucky while we were waiting for somebody to talk to us on the radio.

We knew Crissy had finally gone to the doctor, and had spent some time in the hospital before school went out, but Bucky still didn't know what was wrong with her. Maybe she didn't know either.

"She's better," Bucky said brightly, and smiled. "The doctor's medicine sure works better than that stinkin' stuff she made herself. She's been feeling good enough to help me in the garden."

"That's great news," Lindy said.

"I think maybe she's gonna be okay," he said.

At that moment a voice came on the radio. "I read'ja, Little Bit. This is Roger's Other Woman truckin' down forty-nine, come back."

Roger! We grinned and poked each other.

It was the fad for drivers to invent descriptive names for their trucks. Another time it might be Joe's Dark Dame, Bill's Yellow Babe, or John's Red Ruby. But this was the first Roger we had found. Bucky had been wanting to talk to a Roger just so he could say, "Roger, Roger."

"Seen any smokies today, Other Woman?" I said. "Come back."

"No smokies on the trail. How old you be, Little Bit?"

"Forty-two. How old you be?"

"I be feelin' like a hundred today, Little Bit, come back?"

"A hundred!" Lindy blurted. "Roger, this is Sweet Thang, and I'll declare you're too old to drive, much less have another woman!"

We could hear the trucker laughing, and in the background we could hear Jim Croce singing "Bad, Bad Leroy Brown."

"Where ya goin' to?" Bucky said. "Come back."

"And what's your handle, boy?" Other Woman said.

"This is Boy Wonder," Bucky shot back.

"Hey, Boy Wonder! I be headin' to de hills wid a load of coffin nails."

That meant he was going to Asheville, or maybe Boone, with a truck full of cigarettes.

"You copy?" Roger asked.

"ROGER, ROGER!" Bucky shouted, and we giggled like crazy. When we had settled down some, Bucky added, "You mean you're hauling cancer sticks?"

"For shore! For shore! Winston pays good like a cigarette should!" Other Woman came back.

We knew Roger was saying he didn't care what he was hauling as long as he was well paid. By this time me and Lindy had been made aware of the fact that Bucky detested anything to do with tobacco.

"Bucky Bark wouldn't haul a cigarette across the road if you paid him a million dollars!" Lindy said, forgetting to use Bucky's handle.

"Bucky Bark!" Another voice butted into our conversation. "Boy Wonder, do you belong to Crissy Bark?"

We were startled into silence. Lindy had broken Grandma's rule: don't tell anybody who you are.

"This is Roy's Blue Lady north of Buttermilk Hill," the new trucker hollered. "Boy Wonder, you still got'cha ears on?" He was breaking up.

"That's a big ten-four, good buddy. This is Boy Wonder," Bucky said with not much enthusiasm. "Come back."

"I knew a Crissy Bark in Buttermilk Hill," the trucker went on. "I had a riding partner named Buckroe Silver, and he courted her for a while. I reckon that's been almost fifteen year ago. You belong to Buckroe and Crissy? Come back."

We had all gone into shock. It was awful.

"I'm ridin' outa range," Blue Lady went on. "Anyways, tell Crissy that Roy Stone said hello. Over and out."

"I reckon we got some interference there," Other Woman came back.

But Bucky shut off the CB with his fist, then sat there flushed and breathing hard.

So that's where Bucky got his catchy name, I was thinking. From a trucker. Almost fifteen years ago. Yeah, that would be about right. But what a lousy way to find out who your daddy is.

Without a word, Bucky climbed out of the pickup, hopped onto his bike, and rode away as fast as he could pedal.

23

The following Friday there was no call from Daddy and Melba inviting me for the weekend, and my feelings were not hurt a bit. Saturday found me and Lindy and Bucky together again at the cemetery. Bucky seemed to be over his fury, but Lindy and I decided not to mention the CB or the previous Saturday's conversation with the trucker, unless he brought it up first. He didn't.

Instead he dropped a bomb.

"Did it make you mad when your daddy bought horses for them two boys of his?" he asked me.

"What're you talkin' about?" I said.

"The twins," Bucky said. "Didn't y'all know they got horses?"

Lindy and I were dumbfounded.

"You ain't seen 'em yet?" Bucky said incredulously. "Two big ole golden ones. They look like Trig . . . ger . . ."

Bucky's voice trailed away, and he dropped his eyes.

"Oh, you didn't know," he said.

No, it couldn't be true.

"Tell us," Lindy said.

"I figgered you knew already," he said.

"Tell us," Lindy said again, but I couldn't speak.

"Well, yesterday Marvin Johnson drove me out that way to fetch some manure, and we saw Larry and Lewis riding horses. When Marvin stopped to brag on 'em, the boys said their new daddy bought 'em for 'em."

My eyes began to smart.

"Geez, y'all, I'm sorry I opened my big mouth," Bucky apologized again. "I just thought . . ."

"It's okay, Bucky," Lindy said. "It's not your fault."

As Lindy and I looked at each other, I could see my own pain reflected there in the Berry blue eyes.

"Do they have names?" she said to Bucky.

"Yeah, Tom and Jerry," Bucky said.

Tom and Jerry. What stupid, unimaginative names. Cartoon characters. A cat and a mouse. But you couldn't expect Larry and Lewis to come up with a name as wonderful as Misty or Black Beauty or Velvet, or the names Lindy and I had picked out—Whisper and Sunset.

"I wonder why they said nothing about getting horses when we were there two weeks ago?" Lindy said.

"Yeah, I wonder."

"Maybe they got 'em on the spur of the moment—or maybe it's a surprise!" Bucky said cheerfully. "Yeah, they're prob'ly for y'all, too!"

Good old Bucky.

For the rest of the day Lindy and I were gloomy, and didn't talk much, even to each other. Late in the evening Mama began to pick around on that sorry old guitar, so I went down to the pond by myself.

It was a lazy, quiet evening. The sun was throwing golden ribbons across the surface of the water. I heard a plop like a frog had jumped off his log.

"Old Croaker?" I said out loud, and smiled at the memory of me and him making up rhymes together.

Yeah, I reckon I had outgrown Old Croaker, but I could make up poems by myself now. And as soon as that thought crossed my mind, the first lines of a poem came to me: *Horses' manes flow soft in young girls' dreams . . . seined by fingers of a breeze . . . eyes wild with life . . .*

And the hurt seemed easier to bear.

From the screened-in porch I could hear Mama playing and singing "The Cry of the Wild Goose," and she didn't sound all that bad either.

24

That night I finished my poem, and the next day I gave Lindy a copy of it.

"It's the best one you've ever done, Piper," she said, then added, "Maybe it's 'cause your heart was all the way in it."

"Yeah, maybe."

"You know Miss Penninger, the new town librarian?" Lindy said.

"Yeah, I know her."

"Well, she's having this thing on the first Tuesday night of the month. People go to the library and read stuff out loud to other people."

"What kind of stuff?" I said.

"Things they made up—stories and poems, but none of them are good as yours."

"How do you know? You haven't been there."

"No, but I know nobody in this town can write a poem like you can."

I smiled. When I was just a little kid and wrote nonsense stuff, Mama read my poems. But she hadn't read one in a long time now. Maybe I should share them with her and other people and get different points of view.

"Let's go to the next one," Lindy said, "and you bring this poem to read aloud, okay?"

"Maybe I'll do that," I said. "And maybe I can talk Mama into coming with us."

But Mama had other plans.

"Piper, there's something I want to ask you about," she said that very night.

We were in the living room eating boiled peanuts and tossing the shells in a poke. Rain had cooled the air, and I had my quilt over my bare legs. I looked at Mama and waited.

"Guy has asked me to go to Norfolk, Virginia, with him. My classes are not meeting for a few days because of the Fourth of July, and I'm taking off work."

For about half a second I was thrilled. Wow! I'd love to go to Norfolk, Virginia! But no . . . she didn't say I was invited. What was she saying?

"I wonder," she went on. "I mean . . . do you think you could stay with your dad while I'm gone?"

I looked at the calendar hanging right there on the wall behind the couch.

"What day are you leaving on?" I asked.

"Saturday the third."

"And when are you coming back?"

"The following Wednesday, the seventh."

So she would be in Norfolk on the first Tuesday of the month. I wiped my hands on my shirt and fingered the quilt patches.

Here were pieces of my and Lindy's christening gowns . . . Mama's favorite maternity dress . . . the shirt Daddy wore the night he graduated from high school . . . the tablecloth used at Mama and Daddy's wedding reception.

"I'll stay with Lindy," I said.

"I think you should stay with your daddy and Melba," Mama said. She was not smirking.

"I'll stay with Lindy," I repeated.

"Daddy may not like that," Mama said. "Let's ask him before you decide."

"No, Mama," I said firmly. "Lindy and I have some plans to make."

"Well, okay, if you're sure," Mama said, "but if your daddy gets mad at you, don't blame me."

"He won't get mad," I said. "He won't care a bit."

As if to prove my point, neither Daddy nor Melba called me that last weekend in June. It made me wonder if they were trying to keep the horses a secret from me and Lindy.

When Mama left for Norfolk with Guy, she was all excited, and I reckoned, as hard as she worked, she deserved a vacation.

So I put on a brave face and grinned at her as she waved goodbye from the window of Guy's Karmann Ghia. Then I sighed and walked down to Lindy's.

That evening, when Lindy and I were at the pond, Mrs. Kluttz hollered at me from the back steps of her trailer, "Piper, your telephone is ringing off the hook!"

"Thank you, Mrs. Kluttz!" I yelled back, but I made no move to go.

Mrs. Kluttz didn't give up. "It's the second time it's rung!"

Lindy and I looked at each other and didn't say anything. We had heard the phone and ignored it, because we thought it might be Daddy calling to invite me, maybe both of us, for the Fourth of July.

"You want me to answer it?" Mrs. Kluttz went on doggedly.

"No, ma'am!" I yelled back. "Let it ring!"

She threw up her hands like she was aggravated, and went back into her trailer.

There was a Fourth of July parade that weekend, and it was especially big because it was the Bicentennial.

Leading the parade was the high school band, followed by the fire truck, then Papa, the mayor, riding in Buttermilk Hill's one police car. Behind him came a beauty queen representing the high school, riding on a float made for her by the Jaycees. There were also floats for the 4-H Club, Future Homemakers of America, and Future Farmers of America. Bucky was on that one.

At night Bucky, Lindy, and I watched the fireworks at the high school, and the celebrations were over. I had expected to see Daddy and Melba with their three kids at one of the events, but they didn't show up, and I was relieved.

As the days of Mama's absence went by, I couldn't tell much difference if she was gone or not. Lindy and I tromped in and out of the trailer like always, to get a Popsicle, or a change of clothes, or a drink of water, or coins from the sugar bowl.

The only difference was that I stayed with Lindy at night and Booger had to sleep alone at the trailer. I missed her, and I knew she missed me, too.

Deep in the nights I would wake up and look toward the trailer park, imagining Booger asleep on the cool porch, her golden legs pawing the air, as she dreamed of running after me and Lindy on our bicycles. I might not have a horse, I thought, but I have me the sweetest dog in the world.

25

Tuesday night, after eating supper with Lindy, I went to the trailer and put on my best sundress, which showed off my tan. It was red cotton with one white daisy on the skirt. With it I wore my good white sandals, which I usually saved for church.

I pinned my short blond hair back behind my ears with daisy barrettes. Looking at myself in the mirror, I could see that Lindy and I still looked like twins.

I put Booger on the screened-in porch with food and fresh water, and went back down the path to Lindy's. She told me I looked pretty.

Lindy called Grandma, who was still at the Tarheel, told her where we were going, and we set off for the library, which was right beside the cemetery.

I knew the poem by heart, but I was afraid I might get nervous and forget it, so once again I had written it on a piece of paper. Now I clutched it tight in one hand. Before we got to the library, it was all wrinkled and sweaty.

First we went in the library office to see Miss Penninger. She seemed surprised to see me, but she was nice. She asked me what I was going to read, and then she told me to sit in the first row of chairs she had set up in the main room. There was a podium in front of the chairs.

Lindy and I sat together, and I started sweating as the place filled up behind us. We could hear the laughter and chatter of the townspeople, but I was afraid to turn around and see who was there.

When Miss Penninger got up front to begin the program, I finally peeped around at the others, and I was mortified. Besides me and Lindy, only grownups were there, and they included some schoolteachers.

"Let's get out of here!" I whispered to Lindy.

"No!" she said sternly, clutching my arm. "You got nothing to worry about. Your poem will be the best one."

Right then I saw Dr. Fisher come in the door.

"Get real, Lindy. I'm outa my league. Let's leave!"

"No, Piper. I'm telling you yours will be the best, I know it will!"

I stood up, and was ready to bolt when I heard Miss Penninger calling my name with a great big smile in her voice.

"Piper Berry is going to read for us first."

First? I nearly died. But at this point I saw no way out. Everybody applauded politely and waited for me to walk to the podium and read my poem.

Oh, I get it, I thought, they're indulging me. They want to get me out of the way so they can get on with the real show. Okay, might as well do it. I'll read fast and be gone.

On trembling legs I walked to the podium. It was too high for me, so I stood beside it and read my poem.

"Horses' manes flow soft in young girls' dreams . . ."

I read as fast as I could, then rushed to sit down before anybody could react.

"Okay, now let's get out of here," I whispered to Lindy.

The applause was scattered and polite.

Then, "Read that again, young lady!" Dr. Fisher bellowed. It was a command.

"Yes, do!" Miss Penninger said excitedly. "I don't think I heard it all!"

And the clapping picked up some.

"Again!"

"Read it again!"

"Slow it down a bit."

"Yeah, and louder. We want to hear it all."

So once again I rose before the group, but this time I felt a thrill.

Did they really like my poem? I read it again, slow and clear:

"In Young Girls' Dreams
by Piper Berry (age 13)

"Horses' manes flow soft in young girls' dreams
seined by fingers of a breeze

eyes wild with life, and with flame
never bridled, never named

"And in those sweet dreams wild horses fly
to sleep's stars, to dream-blue skies
lighting on a star they neigh
singing storms and winds away

"In dreams young girls ride by pony fare
fingers twined in their colts' hair
sailing through unwatered seas
gliding through dreams' galaxies

"Riding swift on a thought untethered
freed from rein, free of leather
uncaught, like summer leaves on gentle streams
so flow horses in young girls' dreams"

Now the applause was loud and enthusiastic, and I couldn't hide the grin that came out of me. I sat back down beside Lindy, and she squeezed my arm.

"Is it Denver's girl?" I heard somebody whisper.

"Yeah, Denver and that Berry from Elsewhere. It's their girl."

Somebody tapped me on my shoulder and said, "Where's your mama, Piper?"

"Oh, she's . . ."

But I was saved from explaining as Miss Penninger got up front and started talking.

"I think everybody will agree that was really wonderful. I hope more young people will be encouraged to join our group."

"Yes," Dr. Fisher said. "I think young people should always be here."

"Me too!" came from Delbert Driggs. "This is one place where the generations can come together and share and appreciate each other's talents."

Others mumbled their agreement.

"It's also a place they can get support for their creativity."

"I don't know about y'all, but I'd like to hear Piper's poem again. I thought it was real good."

"Yeah, read it again, Piper."

Unbelievable!

Lindy punched me, and everybody clapped again.

"Come on, Piper."

Elated, I read the poem again, and when I was finished, Miss Penninger asked me if I had another copy so she could keep this one. I had read some of my poems aloud at school, but nobody else had ever liked them enough to brag on them like this, or to want a copy for keeps.

I handed my poem to her and floated back to my seat.

After I sat down that time, Miss Penninger moved on to the next reader. Nobody else had a poem that night, but three people had short stories to read. The first was by Mrs. Dwight Miller, one of the schoolteachers, and I couldn't concentrate on her story at all. My mind was racing back over the last few minutes.

I had been sweating when I first sat down, but now my teeth were chattering, and chills were popping out on my bare arms. Some of it was pure exhilaration, but some of it was caused by the air conditioner, which I was not used to at all. It was pumping out frigid air from a vent right over my head.

Next Miss Thornberry, better known to me and Lindy as the Avon lady, read a funny story about some of the people she ran into on her daily rounds of selling cosmetics. Lindy and I laughed so hard 'cause we recognized nearly everybody in her story, even though she didn't use their real names.

With a great swelling of pride, the thought came to me: these are my people.

When it was Dr. Fisher's turn, he read a long story that held us all spellbound. It was about that night so long ago when his baby was stolen from a cradle by an open window at his house on Apple Hill. The child had not been seen or heard tell of again.

There had been no ransom note, no trail, no clues at all, not even a footprint. Just an empty cradle by an open window. All the newspapers at the time had called it the worst and the most baffling crime in the history of the county.

Even after all this time had passed, the kidnapping of baby Boris Fisher was talked about in whispers. Nobody wanted to upset the good doctor and his wife.

You could have heard a pin drop in that room for the first fifteen minutes, and after that you could hear sniffling. By the time he read the last page, there was not a dry eye among us.

Dr. Fisher sat down and dabbed his own eyes. People patted him on the back and talked softly like they were at a wake. The room had a long-ago feeling about it, like it was that very night of the kidnapping.

"Doc, have you tried to publish that?" someone asked him.

"Yes, I submitted it to *Reader's Digest*. Every month they publish what they call the First Person Award. But I haven't heard anything from them yet."

Then the grownups got all involved in a discussion about imagery and metaphors that I couldn't follow. Besides, I was freezing, so I punched Lindy and whispered, "Let's go." She agreed.

As we tiptoed back past the others, they all turned to me, smiling, and made comments.

"Good job, Piper."

"Y'all be sure and come back next time."

"Keep up the good work."

"You'll always have an audience here."

26

When we reached the front door, I was surprised to see Bucky sitting on the floor behind the checkout desk by the entrance. He had not been visible from the main floor of the library where we had been.

"What'n the world are you doin' there?" I whispered, careful not to disturb the gathering.

He stood as we came up beside him, trying to grin, but I could tell he had been crying.

"I came to walk you home," he whispered back.

As we slipped out the door, the hot air enveloped us like a steam bath, but it felt good after being chilled to the bone by the air conditioner.

"How long were you there?" Lindy asked Bucky.

"The whole time."

"So you heard Piper's poem?"

"Oh, yeah, I heard," Bucky said. "It was super, Piper."

"Did you hear Dr. Fisher's story?"

"Yeah," Bucky said. "That was sad."

"Did it make you cry?" Lindy said.

"Yeah," Bucky said, again in a whisper, and pulled his bicycle out of the shubbery where he had stashed it.

"It made everybody cry," I said.

We walked slowly past the cemetery. It lay sleeping peacefully, its grass and shrubs meticulously manicured, its mounds like piles of winter covers over the cold bones beneath. If you listened carefully, you could hear the white headstones whispering their melancholy stories to the night.

> . . . Dearest angel, Jesus loved you
> and took you home . . .
> . . . Many a flower is born to blush
> unseen and waste its sweetness on the
> desert air . . .

As he pushed his bicycle along beside us, Bucky said, "I was at the hospital earlier, visiting Mama."

"Oh, no!" Lindy said. "Then she's sick again?"

"Yeah, she's real bad this time."

"Do you know yet what's wrong with her?" I asked.

"Cancer," he said softly.

Lindy and I gasped at the same time, but we didn't know what to say. What could we say? I searched my brain. How would I feel if Mama had cancer? What would I want people to say to me? I would want them to tell me it wasn't so, that it was all a big mistake.

"Are they sure about it?" I said.

"Yeah, I reckon she's known it all along. The doctor told me she's been in remission, but now he expects she won't have many more good weeks."

"Does that mean . . . ?" Lindy said, but did not finish the thought.

"Yeah, that's exactly what it means," he said sadly.

The word *death* was not spoken among us, but all three of us glanced back at the cemetery.

I envisioned the two mounds where Crissy's parents were buried. She would probably lie beside them. What would Bucky want to say on her tombstone? Tears suddenly burned my eyes.

"Oh, Bucky, I'm so sorry," I choked.

His shoulders sagged as he whispered. "People gotta die, I reckon. It's part of life."

I remembered Daddy saying that same thing to me and Lindy on that long-ago Sunday when old Mr. Mack fell over and died on me.

"But she's so young," I protested.

"What are you going to do, Bucky?" Lindy said. "I mean after she's gone?"

"What do you mean, what am I going to do?" he said, seeming a bit miffed. "I'll go on living. That's what I'll do!"

"I mean, who will you live with?"

Bucky shuffled his feet. "I dunno."

We passed the old hosiery mill and the Citgo station on Mill Street.

"Maybe I'll try to find that truck driver."

"What truck driver?" Lindy and I said at the same time.

"That Buckroe Silver feller. There's not likely to be more than one person with that name, right?"

"Right," I said with not much enthusiasm. Lindy said nothing.

We reached Lindy's house. Bucky propped his bicycle against the mailbox, and we all collapsed on the porch, sighing, saying nothing. I could hear muffled sounds from the TV inside the house, and I could see Papa's head where he rested it against the back of his favorite chair.

"Do you ever wonder what's out there?" Bucky said.

With his head thrown back, he was looking up at the sky, where millions of stars were winking at us.

"Other worlds," Lindy said. "Maybe one just like ours."

"Stranger things than we have ever dreamed of," I said. "Our imaginations are not big enough."

"Gardens," Bucky said. "It's full of gardens. The gardens of the gods."

His eyes were shining.

"Are we a part of that?" I said.

"Yes, Earth is one of those gardens. We were planted here from seeds that had their beginnings out there. We have exceeded all the expectations of the gods, and when they come back to check on their crops, they will be moved to tears with our . . . our . . ." I watched Bucky search for the right word. "Our magnificence!"

I saw Lindy place one hand lightly on Bucky's arm.

"Such magnificent beings don't ever die," he went on. "They just go to sleep."

"We are such stuff as dreams are made on," I said softly, re-membering Shakespeare's words from the tombstone of Julius Cantor Fritz, *"and our little life is rounded with a sleep."*

When I looked at Bucky again, he was smiling at me through his tears.

27

Muggy July afternoons are the best time for catching bream, and the next day found me and Lindy at the pond, fishing and chatting about the previous night. Bucky was spending the day with Crissy at the hospital.

After about an hour we were surprised to see Daddy coming around the end of the trailer by himself. I realized I had not seen him alone, without Melba and the twins, since the first night he had introduced me to them almost two years ago.

He was wearing jeans, and he stopped to get his cane fishing pole out from under the trailer, where it had been collecting dirt and spiderwebs. He cleaned it off with his shirttail as he came toward us.

"Howdy, girls," he said as he sat down on the grassy bank between us. He baited his hook with one of our crickets and tossed the line in the water. "Anything bitin' today?"

"Yeah, they're bitin' good," I said.

"See?" Lindy said, and showed him our string, which was pegged into the ground beside her.

"Good catch," Daddy said. "Real good. Who taught y'all to fish like that?"

We grinned.

Booger came up to Daddy and tried to be friendly, but he pushed her away.

"Come here, Booger, lay down here," I said, and patted the ground beside me. Obediently, she did as I said, and I petted her.

"She misses Mama," I said.

"Where's she gone to?" Daddy said.

"Gone to Norfolk, Virginia, with Guy," I said.

"And left you all by yourself?" Daddy said crossly.

"I'm not by myself," I said. "I've got Booger, and I'm staying with Lindy."

"Well, you tell your mama I said she should not go off and leave you like that!" he said sternly.

Look who's talking!

I didn't say it out loud, but I guess Daddy was surprised at the way I looked at him.

"What?" he said.

"Nothing," I said with a shrug.

The three of us sat in silence for the longest time.

Then directly Daddy said, "Got one!" and he pulled his line out of the water. A big old golden bream was flopping in the sun.

"Me too!" I hollered, and hauled in my catch as well.

Booger jumped up and wagged her tail. She always congratulated me like that when I caught one. Then she lay back down.

"Why didn't you come stay with us?" Daddy asked as he put his fish on our stringer.

"I had things to do at the library," I said.

"Yeah, that new librarian called me this morning."

"Miss Penninger?" I said.

"Yeah, that's her name. She said that poem you read last night was really something."

I smiled, pleased, as I strung my fish behind Daddy's.

"Dr. Fisher called me, too," he added.

"Dr. Fisher?" Lindy and I sputtered together.

"Yeah, he went on and on about how good that poem was, how I should encourage your writing, make sure you get a good education, and all that stuff."

Dr. Fisher!

"Then Lucy Harkey called and said, 'That li'l ole Piper's not big as a minute, but she wrote a poem as pretty as any you'd find in a book.' It seems like everybody's heard that poem but me."

"Mama hasn't either," I said.

"Everybody but your mama and daddy," Daddy said.

I could have recited it for him right then and there, but he didn't ask me to, so I didn't offer. We were both quiet as we re-baited our hooks.

"I had the strangest dream about you the other night, Piper," Daddy said as he tossed his line back into the water.

I tossed mine in a few feet away from his, and waited for him to go on.

"I dreamed you were outside our new house trying to look

in the window. You were all wrapped up in that old quilt your grandma made you, and you were trying not to be seen out there.

"I thought and thought about what that dream could mean, and I've come to the conclusion that it means you feel left out at my place. You're on the outside looking in, and you feel like you're not a part of the family, right?"

Way to go, Sherlock! was the thought that shot through my head. But I couldn't say that to Daddy. And it occurred to me that when something was really bothering me, I had never in my life told Daddy about it. I felt he wouldn't understand, but now he was asking me to do that, to open up to him.

I shrugged. "Yeah, sometimes."

"You shouldn't feel that way," he said quickly, and for some reason that made me absolutely furious.

I shouldn't feel that way? Like there was something wrong with my feelings? Like it was all my fault?

Then I understood why I had never opened up to Daddy. He didn't listen. And if he did listen, he wouldn't get it. He just wouldn't get it!

"Yeah, I know," I said sarcastically. "I'll try to do better."

But Daddy didn't catch the sarcasm. He didn't catch anything.

"Good," he said. "You do that."

Then he looked at his watch and stood up to go.

"I gotta go pick Melba up. She's at the Curl Up and Dye."

"Bye," I said quickly.

"Larry and Lewis's team is playing against a Salisbury team tomorrow. Do you want to go to the game with us?"

"No," I said. "I don't."

Daddy put his hands on his hips and looked at me hard.

"Why not?"

"I'm not interested in baseball," I said.

"Well, you could get interested," he snapped, "if you wanted to."

"I doubt it," I said.

I could feel him standing there glaring at me, but I kept my eyes on the cork in the water.

Directly he said, "Well, tell your mother—"

But I didn't let him finish.

"Tell her yourself!"

"What's your problem?" he shot back.

Dead silence followed. Even the wild things seemed to hush.

Finally, as if there was nothing left to discuss, Daddy said, "Well, I gotta go. I guess you'll call me when you're ready to come back for a visit?"

"Yeah," I mumbled, but the way I felt right then, I didn't plan to ever call him for any reason.

Then he was gone, and he had not mentioned the poem again. He still had not even heard it, or asked for a copy.

Lindy, who had remained silent through the whole conversation, was now muttering angrily to herself, not so much about what Daddy said, but about what he didn't say.

"He didn't say one word about those horses!" she sputtered. "I wonder why not? Is he trying to keep them a secret from us? Does he think we will never find out?"

28

Mama came back from Virginia tired and cranky, and we both went to bed early. The next morning, as she was about to leave for school and I was in my bedroom dressing, the phone rang and Mama answered it. After her conversation, Mama popped her head into my room. Her eyes were shining.

"Piper, I had no idea. I am so proud of you for getting up in front of all those people. Miss Penninger said your poem was wonderful. Can I see it?"

"Miss Penninger exaggerates," I said, but at the same time I was grinning, and blushing, too, I guess.

"Does she now?" Mama said with a laugh. "I don't think so. She said everybody loved it."

I didn't have another copy of the poem, except in my head, so I recited it for her right then and there, and Mama loved it as well. She hugged me tight before she went out the door.

• • •

Bucky's mama came home from the hospital after a few more days, and we didn't see much of him for a while. He spent much of his time with Crissy. Their neighbors helped by taking turns sitting with Crissy and doing what needed to be done around the house.

One day Mama told me that Miss Penninger had sent my poem to a friend of hers in Chapel Hill, a teacher at a boarding school called Wolfe House, named for the famous North Carolina writer Thomas Wolfe.

We were both sitting at the bar, after dinner.

"It's a very small special school for young writers and poets like you," Mama explained to me. "It's affiliated with the University of North Carolina at Chapel Hill, which has one of the best creative writing programs in the country."

What was she getting at?

"Anyway, Miss Penninger's friend, Amy Landers, works with young poets at the school. She would like to see some more of your poems."

"What for?"

"To see if she thinks you might qualify for Wolfe House."

A boarding school? Was Mama trying to get rid of me? So she could marry Guy and have another baby?

"You mean go there and live?" I hollered. "Leave Buttermilk Hill?"

"You don't have to," Mama said. "It's just a thought. You may not even qualify."

"What do you have to do to qualify?"

"Eventually you'll have to fill out an application," Mama said nonchalantly, like she was not really interested, but she was.

I knew she was making a great effort not to be pushy. "But Miss Landers wants to see more poems now. Do you have any more?"

I left the bar and went to the couch, curled up in my corner, and thought about it. Maybe I could send in some poems just to see what that teacher thought of them. But I would never go to a boarding school.

"Who would pay for it?" I said.

"Oh, it's by scholarship only. The state pays. It's a special magnet school, something like the North Carolina School of the Arts in Winston-Salem, only this one is for young people who show some promise in writing, instead of performing."

"So I guess you'd have to have good grades?" I said.

"Yours are probably good enough," Mama said. "They are more focused on talent than on grades."

"I don't think I'm interested," I said, trying to be as non-chalant as Mama, "but I do have another poem you can give to Miss Penninger."

I went into my room and brought out a new poem. Mama was the first to read it.

The Wild Girl
by Piper Berry (age 13)

Once I thought
Once I knew
Once I dreamed
    That I could see her.
By my window
Late at night

When darkness lay upon
The deepest green of silent water
And the endless gray of sky.
        I could see her.
        The Wild Girl
She was the earth, both fleeting and forever.
Covered in
                Mud from the ponds
                And leaves from the mud
                Covered with shame and yearning and hope.

        But I could see her.
        The Wild Girl
            I could hear her soft and gentle voice
            I saw her ageless, trusting eyes
            I felt her lonely, weeping heart.

        So I reached out my hand
        To bring her in, to wipe the dirt from her
            face and the pain
        From her memory—
        To show her the beauty that only wisdom brings.

        And when I awoke, I could only wonder
        If I thought
        Or if I knew—
        Or if I had dreamed—
            Of the Wild Girl who had disappeared.
            Of the Wild Girl who is me.

29

One evening Bucky called to ask me and Lindy to meet him at the cemetery the next morning. He said he had something important to tell us. He was already there when Lindy and I arrived. We all sat down on the edge of a tombstone that was shaped like three steps. Bucky was clearly agitated.

"Ya'll know that paper I told you about?" he said right away. "The one Mama used to write on at night, and then lock up in a box?"

We nodded.

"I snuck the lockbox outside yesterday and broke it open and read what she wrote."

"Really?" Lindy's voice was an excited whisper. "What did it say?"

Bucky reached into his pocket and pulled out some folded papers.

"This is it," he said. "I've got to let somebody else read it just to make sure it's real and not a dream."

Eagerly I reached for the paper, but he pulled it to his chest protectively.

"First you both got to promise—promise with all your heart that you will never tell no matter what, until I say it's okay to tell."

"Promise," Lindy and I said together, and reached for the paper again. I was about to bust with curiosity.

"I am serious," Bucky said in a very solemn tone. "More serious than I have ever been. This is a sacred promise you are making to me. If you don't think you can keep it, then don't say so."

"I promise," Lindy and I said together, but more seriously this time.

"I will never tell," I said.

"Me neither," Lindy said.

"Until I say you can tell," Bucky added.

"Right, until you say it's okay," I said.

With that Bucky handed the paper to me. It was worn and dirty, almost coming apart where it had been refolded so many times. As I opened it carefully, I saw that it was actually four sheets of legal-size paper with writing on both sides of each sheet. With our heads together, Lindy and I read.

Spring 1976

My dear son, Bucky. This is for your eyes after I am dead and buried in the ground. It's my last will and testament. This old house was give to me by my folks when they died. I never had nobody else. Now it's yours with everything in it for what it's worth to you.

Here is also the truth I should of told long time ago, but I was too hard headed. It's about where you come from.

When I was young I worked for a summer at the Tarheel, and that's where I met a truck driver by the name of Buckroe Silver. He was good lookin and full of charm. I fell in over my head cause nobody ever liked me before. When I found myself in the family way, I was the happiest girl in the world. I started dreaming about being married to Buckroe Silver and us having ourselfs a little baby. I didn't care if it was a boy or a girl. I already loved that baby no matter what it was. But when Buckroe Silver found out about the baby, he disappeared and I never saw him agin. Seems like he already had hisself a family in Virginia and didn't need another. I was heartsick for a little while. Then I started pinning all my hopes and dreams on that baby. Lordy, I had so many plans it was a sight.

Then the baby come to me. He was borned at home a bit premature, but he seemed as healthy as anybody's baby. He looked exactly like his daddy and that's why I named him like I did—Buckroe Silver Bark. I was as happy as a girl like me could ever hope to be.

Buckroe Silver Bark was less than a week old when he started to having breathing problems, but I was a good mother. I took good care of my boy. I used old family remedies to make him breathe better. But then one night the old remedies didn't work. My baby's breath was more and more struggled, and I was scared. I didn't have a telephone, so I ran next door, and I told my neighbor, Susie Hill, you remember her, she used to live behind us in that teeny green house. She was a mean and spiteful woman, but I didn't know it right then. I ask her to call Dr. Fisher for me, tell him to come right away and look after my baby.

Then I waited for Dr. Fisher to come. I won't go into detail. I'll just say that little baby boy died right there in my arms. I was so filled with grief and sorrow, I couldn't even move for the longest time. I just sat there holding him. Dr. Fisher never did come, and after while I started getting mad, and blaming it on him. I said to myself if he had come, he could of saved my baby. He would still be alive. But he didn't come. I thought it was probly cause I had no money. And I was so mad. I hated him so much that I walked all the way to Dr. Fisher's house to cuss him out, and tell him what he had done. It was pretty late when I got there, maybe midnight. I saw lights on at the back of the house, so I went round there to knock on the door. But just before I reached the door, I heard a baby making baby noises, not exactly crying, but getting ready to, you know how new borns do. Well, maybe you don't. Anyhow, I thought maybe my grief was making me hear things. I looked in the window closest to me, and right there on the other side of the window screen, next to a dim lamplight, was Dr. Fisher's newborn baby boy just home from the hospital. And nobody was near him. I just stood and stared, and the idea come to me.

I'd show Dr. Fisher. I'd show him how it feels to lose your little bitty baby. It took me no time at all to remove the screen and lift that baby right out the window. I made no noise at all. And I went on back home and about my business.

That baby was you, Boris Fisher, who I've called Bucky all these years. I burried my own little baby Bucky in the woods out back of our house near an old rotten log.

I figured I would be caught for shore. Nobody was more surprised than me when nobody ask me a single solitary question. I thought surely somebody would figger it out and come take you back to the doctor, but the town settled back down after the big "kidnapping," and I don't think I was even suspected for a minute by anybody. I was stunned with my good fortune. I felt like I really had my baby back.

When I had you with me about a week Susie Hill come over one night and knocked on the door. I ask her in, but she stood on the porch, looking shame faced. Said she come to see if my baby was better. I told her you was the pitcher of health. She said she was glad to hear it. That's when she told me she never called Dr. Fisher for me at all. She said she was mad at me for having a boy when all she had was girls. So just for spite she didn't call the doctor. Said she figgered I was exaggerating anyhow bout how sick my baby was. But now she wanted to fess up.

When she told me that, I wanted to yell at her don't you know what you done? But I couldn't speak. I wanted to hit her right between the eyes. I can't even tell you how bad I wanted to hurt that mean woman. But I was no Miss Innocent my own self. So I just told her to get out of my house. I slammed the door in her face and never spoke to her again.

You have a birthmark, shaped like an hourglass, right on the top of your head. It was plain when you were tiny, and I kept little caps on you. People used to dress babies like that.

Then when you got older, your hair come in thick and black, like Dr. Fisher's, and covered the birthmark.

For all these years I have been amazed that I got away with stealing a baby. As time went by, I loved you more and more. I couldn't have loved my own Bucky any more. Yet I grew sorrier and sorrier that I had done it, and more afraid that somebody would find out. Sometimes, I thought of how I cheated you, and I thought how you might look at me when you discovered what I did to you. It's plain you would have a better life with the Fishers. But I was too big a coward to turn myself in. The guilt has just about drove me crazy. I know you have seen me get crazier and crazier.

With all this eating and eating away at me, it has gnawed into my innards and give me cancer. I am not long for this world. So when you read this letter, you will know the truth. I hope you can find it in your heart to forgive me. Have a good life. With all my love, Crissy Bark.

30

To say that Lindy and I were stunned would be a huge understatement. At first we couldn't even speak, and when we could, we babbled.

Bucky Bark was the long-lost kidnapped son of Dr. Fisher—Boris Fisher!

We cried a little and laughed a little and shook our heads a whole lot. We tried to hug Bucky, but he brushed us off irritably.

"None of that, now," he said.

We went back over the letter, reading and rereading. Then we just sat there staring at each other.

"I was ashamed of her," Bucky said. "Course, you knew that. But I loved her. She was the only mother I'd ever known. I was ashamed of her appearance, of the way she acted and talked in public. People stared at her, and I pretended not to be with her.

"That was mean and hateful of me. She did everything she

could for me. She was raised up poor by backward folks. She could never make money 'cause she didn't have much schooling. But she was good-hearted. And her conscience hurt her real bad. I can see it all now. Whenever we saw the Fishers, she'd get out of sight as quick as—"

"When are you going to tell them?" I interrupted him excitedly. I wanted to be there when it happened.

"I'm not telling anybody anything," Bucky said emphatically. "Not yet, anyway. That's why I made you promise to keep quiet."

"Why not?" I said. "Aren't you about to bust?"

"Think about all the gossip," Bucky said. "And Mama sick as she is."

"But—"

"But nothing. She's still my mama. She's dying, for crying out loud, and she's gonna be my mama until she dies. I won't let anybody bring shame down on her."

"You want her to die in peace," Lindy said with understanding.

"Yeah, I'll tell her that I know, and that I forgive her. But nobody else must know until after her funeral."

"Bucky, the law will have to know," Lindy said.

"Yeah, they will," Bucky agreed, "but they've waited for fourteen years, they can wait a while longer, don't you think?"

"And the Fishers should know as soon—" I began.

But Bucky interrupted me. He was ticked off. "Maybe I shouldn't a' told y'all. Maybe I'm expecting too much of you not to tell."

Lindy and I looked at each other. We did promise.

"She wasn't in her right mind," Bucky said in defense of Crissy, and the thought came to me if Bucky could forgive her, then other people would have to. After all, he was the one most affected.

"I've had nothing else on my mind for twenty-four hours," Bucky said, rubbing his temples like they hurt. "And I try to imagine how . . . how bleak things must have been for her that night. Her little baby died. All her dreams were shattered, and there was nobody there to help her through it.

"She was desperate," he went on. "She was irrational. It was a bad thing to do, but don't you see, her pain was eating her alive? She did it to stop the pain."

"Yes, you have to forgive her," Lindy said softly.

"We won't tell," I said. "We promise."

"That's right," Lindy said. "We won't break our promise to you, Bucky, I mean . . . Boris?"

"No, you gotta call me Bucky all the time just like always."

"Even after . . . ?"

"Yeah, always. It's the only name I've ever known. Besides . . . Boris?"

He made a face, then smiled that cocky sideways smile as he peered out from under a shock of dark hair—just like Dr. Fisher often did. Of course! Why did I never see it before? Why did nobody see it? Because nobody was looking for it.

31

Each member of the Berry family raised a big garden every year, and late in the month of August the harvest brought in more tomatoes, butter beans, and corn than all of us together could eat. That meant Brunswick Stew time.

We always made it on a Saturday when most everybody was off from work. The Tarheel waitresses, Sally and Judith, minded the store while all the Berrys gathered out back where Grandma and Papa had three great big black pots, and fire pits for hanging them over. We would arrive there about six in the morning to get an early start, because it took nearly all day to cook the stew to perfection. When finished, it would be stored in the Tarheel freezer, where the whole family could have access to it for as long as it lasted.

Since the divorce, Mama didn't come to the Brunswick Stew anymore, but Daddy, Melba, Larry, and Lewis had started coming last year, before the wedding, and this year they proudly added baby Laurie to the party. She was almost four months old and just as cute as a button.

Since Lindy and I couldn't help going on and on about Bucky's secret to each other, we agreed to push it to the back of our minds at least for this time with the family. We would not take a chance of being overheard. We were determined to keep our promise to Bucky.

It was a day for being happy. Lindy and I started singing, and Grandma hummed along with us as she scalded and plucked feathers off the freshly killed chickens. Papa also whistled in tune as he began to grind the roast beef into hamburger.

We first helped Aunt JoAnn and Aunt Kay dip the tomatoes into boiling water for a few seconds so the skins would come off easy. Then we started shucking corn.

Larry and Lewis were ordered to shell butter beans into a dishpan. Lindy winked at me because that was a job we didn't like, and we had always had to do it before.

Daddy got the fires started while Uncle Jake and Uncle Tim hauled out the black pots and began to scrub away a year's worth of accumulated nastiness. Finally Grandma tossed in the first ingredient, which was chicken, and the cooking began.

At lunchtime the picnic table was spread with a clean cloth from the Tarheel, and sandwich stuff was laid out. Lindy and I fixed ourselves banana and peanut butter sandwiches, and settled on a couple of Pepsi crates to eat them.

There was a lag in the conversation when the eating got serious. We could hear the summer insects and the birds calling out to one another. They were probably saying, "Free food!"

Then in the lull I heard somebody say, "Hey, Piper, why don't you recite that famous poem for us while we're eating?"

It was Aunt JoAnn.

"Yeah, do," Melba said. "We haven't heard it yet."

"Yeah, come on, Piper," came from Grandma.

Lindy elbowed me. "Go on."

Everybody was looking at me, so I stood up, and they cheered. Then they watched me and waited politely as they ate.

"'In Young Girls' Dreams,'" I said the title, then stopped to clear my throat. "'Horses' manes flow soft in young girls' dreams . . .'"

I was nearly finished with my recitation, when, without warning, I was almost overcome with the deep emotion that had inspired its writing in the first place.

Daddy was my own flesh-and-blood father, and he had laughed when I asked him for a horse, yet he had bought one each for his adopted sons. It was because they were boys. Somehow that made them more worthy.

I felt my face glow hot with the anger and the pain of it. My voice faltered. I looked at Lindy. She winked. So I recited the rest of the poem directly to her.

"'. . . uncaught, like summer leaves on gentle streams, so flow horses in young girls' dreams.'"

This applause seemed extra nice, extra warm because it was from my family. When I finally stole a glance at Daddy, he was standing by one of the black pots, quietly watching me as he stirred the Brunswick stew with a long wooden ladle to keep it from sticking. Larry was on one side of him, and Lewis on the other.

Afterward I couldn't help noticing how Daddy and Melba were glum. I also noticed that Aunt Kay, Aunt JoAnn, and Grandma were mad as fire about something. Then Grandma marched right up to Daddy boldly and said something that appeared to make him uncomfortable.

Shortly thereafter Melba rounded up the children and they left with Daddy without saying goodbye to anybody.

"What happened?" I whispered to Lindy.

"Everybody's mad at Denver," Lindy said with a chuckle.

"About what?" I said.

"About the horses," she went on. "Your poem reminded them just how mean it was for Denver to buy those horses for the twins, and leave you out."

At first I felt wickedly gleeful, vindicated. But before long a heaviness was weighing on my heart. This was worse than before, I thought, because now everybody felt bad, and there was no victory in that.

32

The next day it rained, and Lindy and I were sitting in our booth at the Tarheel after church. We had finished a Sunday dinner of chicken and dumplings, and were deeply engrossed in reading aloud to each other from *The Black Stallion,* when suddenly Daddy was standing there beside our table.

"Lindy," he said in a soft voice, "will you excuse me and Piper for a minute? We got some talking to do."

Lindy left without a word, and Daddy sat down across from me. He rubbed the back of his head. He looked out the window beside us. He flipped through the jukebox selections. He bent over and pretended to tie his shoelaces. Then he looked at me.

"Melba has her own money," he said at last.

"That's nice for her," I said.

"She bought the horses for Larry and Lewis with her own money. All I did was deliver them. I tried to tell her not to do it. I swear I did.

"I told her, I said, 'Melba, these boys are city kids at heart.

They don't need no horses. They'd rather have dirt bikes or mopeds or something like that. They'll lose interest in horses in no time.' But she wouldn't listen."

I found myself saying, "That's okay, Daddy."

"You and Lindy are welcome to come out and ride the horses any time you want to. Last night Melba made the boys agree to that."

She made them? Well, whoop-dee-do. Wadn't that nice of her?

"Like I said, it was Melba's idea to buy the horses," he went on, "but that's no excuse. I've thought and thought about this thing, and I know now where I went wrong."

Daddy changed position two or three times.

"I shoulda told her if we were going to have horses, one of them had to be for you."

Suddenly it was clear to me who was boss at the new house.

"One for you and Lindy and one for Larry and Lewis. That woulda been the fair thing."

I nodded in agreement.

"But it's too late now," Daddy said. "I can't take one of them away and say it's yours. I'm trying to say I made a mistake, Piper, and I don't know how to fix it. I hurt you, I know that now, and I was wrong, but I don't know how to make it right."

"Well, that's okay," I said again, because I didn't know what else to say.

"No, it is not okay, Piper. I know it's not okay, you know it's not okay, Mom and Papa and JoAnn and Jake and Kay and Tim, and everybody else in Buttermilk Hill, knows it's not okay. I messed up big time."

From the jukebox at that moment Michael Martin Murphey

started belting out "Wildfire," which was about a horse. I heard every word, but I don't think Daddy even noticed what was playing.

"I would buy another horse for you," he went on, "but we don't have enough stalls, and there's not room to build another one. And God knows, we can't afford to feed the ones we got."

Besides, Melba won't let you, I was thinking.

But again I said, "That's okay."

He let out a long, heavy sigh.

"I guess I dropped the ball when I left you and your mother." He rubbed the back of his head again. "I neglected you."

I started to say "That's okay" again, but thought better of it.

"It just seemed that when you started growing up, I didn't have anything in common with you anymore. You have always been exactly like your mama."

Then he added quickly, "Not that there's anything wrong with that. You've been a good girl, Piper, a real good girl. You've never given me or your mama a minute's trouble."

I rolled the salt shaker between my palms, and Daddy started playing around with the sugar packets.

"Don't you have anything to say?" he said at last.

Of all the times I had visualized myself telling Daddy and Mama exactly what I thought of them, I knew I never would do any such a thing.

My mind went back to that moment when I was listening to Mama and Daddy fight on his last night with us. The memory used to be like an open cut on your finger that won't close up and everything gets in it and makes it hurt. But over time it had turned into an ordinary ache.

I sat up straight and looked into Daddy's eyes. They were sad.

I took a deep breath and said, "The night you went away, I heard you say to Mama, 'We have our children and they have their children, and that's all there is.'"

"Yeah, I remember saying that."

"Well, I've thought about that, Daddy. I've thought and thought a lot."

"And what have you come up with?"

"I don't think that's all there is. I think dreams are important, too."

He nodded, and I was surprised he didn't argue with me.

"And I think you and Mama both would've been happier people if you had gone after your own dreams before you got married."

"You may be right, Piper," he said very softly.

"You gave up on your dreams, but that didn't mean Mama had to give up on hers."

Daddy sighed. "But it's too late to do anything about any of that now, Piper."

"I know, Daddy. I know it's too late for y'all. But it's not too late for me. My dreams are as important as anybody's. Just because I'm not a boy and a baseball player, don't think I'm not important."

We sat looking at each other then, and I saw my daddy's eyes actually fill up with tears!

"I don't think that at all, Piper," he said at last. "I know I haven't shown it lately, but you are important to me, very important. And I am going to do better. I promise."

That's when a great flood of joy rushed through me, for suddenly I saw what I had done, and I was so proud I almost burst. Without making accusations or showing jealousy, without whining or hollering at anybody, I had finally made somebody hear me.

And I had done it with a poem.

The next Friday Daddy picked me and Lindy up and took us to the country for the weekend. I had to admit that Melba had always been good to me, but now she seemed even more eager to please both me and Lindy. And the twins went out of their way to be friendly.

Maybe it was just me, I thought. Maybe it was my attitude that had changed because I wanted to work things out with Daddy. Or maybe it was both me and Daddy, and our new attitude toward each other affected the whole family. Whatever it was, everybody was happier.

We met the horses on Friday evening, and took turns riding them around the yard and barnyard. Then on Saturday morning Larry and Lewis offered to let me and Lindy ride by ourselves through the woods and rolling farmlands in back of the house.

That's how Lindy and I had our first experience with Tom and Jerry in the warm September sunshine. With a light breeze in our hair and a fire in our eyes, we got to know and love these two beautiful creatures. They were wonderfully gentle, and well trained. After that we looked forward to going to the country almost every weekend.

33

On a cold October day, with wet leaves clinging to our shoes, we stood in a light rain with Bucky in the cemetery. Lucerne's Funeral Home was conducting Crissy Bark's funeral, and doing a good job of it, even though they might never see a penny for it.

Bucky stood hunched over in a borrowed navy suit that was too big for him. He had not spoken that day. Even when Lindy and I had put our arms around him, trying to console him, he looked away, and shivered.

"'In my Father's house are many mansions,'" Reverend Rivers was reading from the Bible. "'If it were not so, I would have told you. I go to prepare a place for you.'"

Bucky raised his head to give attention to the minister's words.

"Do you think it's so?" he muttered as he was climbing into June Bug with me and Mama and Lindy after the service.

"What?" I said. "Is what so?"

"What the Reverend said?"

"Which part?"

"Many mansions—that part."

"Yes, I do, Bucky. The Bible says many mansions are there, and I think your mama—Crissy—will get one for herself."

"And the real Bucky Bark, too?" he whispered.

"Definitely. They will get one together."

Bucky settled into the backseat with me as Lindy climbed into the front with Mama. He closed his eyes. We rode in silence to the Tarheel, where we were going for dinner.

Grandma gave us a table that was usually reserved for a large party of paying customers. She brought out fried chicken and mashed potatoes and gravy, all family style, with hot biscuits and butter, green veggies, and chocolate cake. It was akin to her special Sunday dinner. Then she sat down and ate with us.

We kept the conversation light during the meal, but Bucky remained quiet and thoughtful. Even though he rarely saw a spread like this, he barely picked at his food, and didn't take dessert when it was offered.

"Where are you staying tonight?" Mama asked him when we had finished eating.

"At home," was all he said.

"By yourself?" Mama said.

"Sure, I stayed there alone every time Mama was in the hospital. The neighbors look in on me, and bring me stuff."

"But you can't go on doing that," Grandma said gently.

"No, I won't," Bucky answered. "I've got plans."

Several families in town had offered to take him in, but he always answered, "I've got plans." Today it wasn't enough for Grandma.

"We have an extra bedroom at our house," she said to him at this point, and everybody at the table showed surprise. She, too, was offering Bucky a home?

"That's mighty kind of you, Miz Berry," he answered her politely. "But believe me, I do have plans. Don't you worry."

"Well, you have to let us know what your plans are, Bucky," Grandma said firmly. "I worry about you. You can't live alone."

"I know, and I'll let you know soon, Miz Berry," he answered her. "I . . . I'll let everybody know. I promise."

At that point he glanced at me and then at Lindy and bit his lip, but he wasn't smiling. He seemed worried. Out the window we could see the rain was coming down in sheets.

We drove Bucky to Tacky Town and let him out in front of the tiny house Crissy had left him. He forgot to say thank you and good night before he bolted through the rain and disappeared into the house. But a touch of forgetfulness was easily forgiven in these circumstances.

We didn't see Bucky again for several days, and Lindy and I could hardly stand the suspense. Then he showed up at the Tarheel on a gorgeous Sunday afternoon, appearing freshly bathed and combed and dressed in clean clothes. Lindy and I were finishing up lunch, and we waved him to our table. He came toward us smiling nervously.

He sat down with us, and Judith appeared to take his order. "What'll it be, Bucky?"

"Nothing, thanks, Judith. I ate with the Johnsons today. We had black-eyed peas, collard greens, and pork chops."

"Well, we can't top that!" Judith said with a smile, and left our table.

Lindy and I managed to hold our tongues until he was ready to say what he had to say. We had decided not to be pushy, and not to beg him to let us witness the big event.

"I'm going to do it today." The words spilled out of him. "I have to get it over with."

"You're going over there?" Lindy said breathlessly.

"I was wondering . . ." he began.

"Wondering what?" I said.

"Well, actually I'm scared," he confided.

"Scared of what?" from Lindy.

"Suppose they don't believe me? Suppose they tell me to get out of their house or something, and quit bothering them?"

"You have the letter, don't you?"

"Yeah." Bucky patted his shirt pocket. "But that's not proof."

I noticed his fingernails were chewed down to the quick, and there were dark circles under his eyes.

"Bucky," I said, "I think they are going to be so overjoyed that they—they won't know what to do."

"They won't doubt you for a minute," Lindy agreed. "This will answer all the questions they've been worrying over for years. It will make sense to them now."

"I was wondering if y'all would go with me?" he said quietly.

"Yes!" we squealed together, and some of the customers turned to stare at us.

"Right now?" he said hopefully.

"Yes!" we squealed again.

In less than five minutes we were on our bicycles, pedaling as fast as we could toward Dr. Fisher's house on Apple Hill.

34

"*Well, what have we here?*"

Dr. Fisher, his own self, answered the door, when we rang the doorbell.

Bucky had rehearsed what he was going to say, but now that he was face to face with the good doctor, he couldn't utter a syllable.

The silence was awkward, so Lindy said, "We have something to show you, Dr. Fisher. Do you think we could come in?"

"Why, certainly, Lindy, certainly! Come in. What's this all about? Nobody's sick, I hope?"

Dr. Fisher flung the door wide open and ushered us inside. He was still wearing his church clothes, except for his jacket and tie.

"No, nobody's sick," Lindy said.

"I'm glad to hear that!"

Lindy and I sat down on an attractive brown leather couch as the doctor sat in an armchair nearby and crossed his hands over his ample tummy. He studied us curiously. His dark hair was hanging down in his eyes, just like Bucky's did, and they had the same eyes.

Bucky remained standing and staring at the doctor.

"You're the Bark boy, right?" Dr. Fisher said to him.

Bucky nodded.

"I was sorry to hear about your mother. Won't you have a seat?"

Bucky perched on the sofa between me and Lindy. Still he didn't speak up. I poked him with my elbow. He didn't move, but I saw that a tear had started rolling down the side of his face.

"Mrs. Fisher and the girls are visiting relatives in Raleigh this weekend," Dr. Fisher said. "So I have the house all to myself. The place seems bigger when you're rattling around in it by yourself. Know what I mean?"

Nobody spoke.

The doctor looked from one of us to another. "You said you have something to show me?"

Bucky leapt from his seat. "Never mind," he said loudly. "It's not important. Just—never mind."

Lindy grabbed his pants leg and pulled him back down beside her. "Don't back out now. Show him the letter."

Now the doctor was really curious. You could see it in his eyes.

"Letter?" he said.

With trembling fingers Bucky reached into his shirt pocket and pulled out the battered letter. The doctor rose from his chair and took the letter from Bucky's hand. Then he unfolded the paper and adjusted his glasses.

As we watched the doctor reading, there was no sound except for Bucky's heavy breathing. Dr. Fisher's eyes traveled down the first page quickly, eagerly. Then he turned it over and read the back page. His lips began to move slightly as he read.

As he read on, his face went white, and he collapsed into the armchair as if there were no bones in his body.

He looked at Bucky then, and his gaze was piercing.

"You . . . ?" he said.

Bucky nodded. His face was wet, and scared.

Dr. Fisher finished the letter, then read the whole thing through again, while Bucky sat there silently twisting his hands together. It was agonizing.

"Oh, my God!" the doctor said then. "Nobody knew about the birthmark. It was never published in the papers. Oh, my dear God!"

He stood up again, as if sitting still was impossible for him.

"You . . . ?" he repeated.

It occurred to me suddenly that this news might give Dr. Fisher a heart attack or something. He did not look well at all.

"I would have helped her," he said. "In fact, I offered to deliver her baby. But she said she couldn't pay. She was ashamed to take charity. Still, I would have tried to save her baby that night if I had been called."

Bucky bolted to his feet, and words about his mother began tumbling out. "I don't want you to hate her! She was not in her right mind. She was crazy with grief. But she was always good to me. She loved me and I loved her."

His tears were flowing, but he went on and on about their life together, about her sacrifices and her guilt.

"Oh, my boy, my boy," Dr. Fisher interrupted him at last. Now his tears were flowing, too, and Lindy and I were far from dry-eyed. "You are restored to us. At this moment that's all that matters."

With these words he reached for Bucky, and Bucky went into his arms. They stood there together crying, and no more words needed to be said.

35

Spreading the big news was the frosting on the cake for me and Lindy. As we watched people's mouths fall open with shock and surprise, we felt important. Within hours everybody in Buttermilk Hill knew that the mystery of Boris Fisher had been solved. The next day the town was invaded with reporters and photographers and policemen. It was weeks before life in Buttermilk Hill was normal again.

Bucky and the Fishers had to adjust to each other, and that was not easy. With Crissy, Bucky had always been free to come and go as he pleased. Now he didn't have that freedom. But for Bucky, security was the trade-off. The center of much attention for the first time in his life, he was able to spend hours with his family, getting to know them and all the relatives.

He was also dressed and groomed in an appropriate manner for the son of a doctor. He found that money for his college education had been set aside in the event that he returned to home and hearth. And that having a farmer in the family was perfectly acceptable to the Fishers.

My application to Wolfe House arrived in February, and was stuffed into a drawer in my bedside table. Occasionally I looked at it and put it away again. To be admitted for the coming school year, I had to meet the application deadline by the end of March.

Larry and Lewis had lost interest in Tom and Jerry, like Daddy had predicted they would, and they allowed us to rename the horses. Next thing we knew, everybody was referring to Whisper as Piper's horse and Sunset as Lindy's.

Daddy actually let us bring Booger with us when we visited, and the twins fell in love with her, so they became our allies in sneaking her into the house at night. Melba knew what we were doing, but she didn't tell Daddy.

Larry and Lewis no longer complained about giving up their beds when we spent the night. In fact, Lindy, Booger, and I gradually took over Larry's room, as he moved his belongings, a few at a time, into Lewis's room.

Guy Webb didn't come around much anymore, and Mama was too busy to miss him, as she started her student teaching in the county schools. It involved music instruction to all the grades, kindergarten through high school. She was nervous, and spent a lot of time with lesson plans for all those age groups.

She had to limit the hours she worked at Mum's to weekends only, but she hoped to get a teaching position so she could quit Mum's for good.

One evening in early March, as we were eating supper, Mama said, "Piper, I need to know soon what you plan to do about applying to Wolfe House."

I shrugged. "I don't think I'm going to apply."

"Why not?"

"I don't want to leave home."

Mama smiled warmly at me.

"Well, here's why I'm asking—I have tried not to push you because I know you might be homesick, and I don't want you to think I am trying to get rid of you either. But I want so much for you to have this opportunity. You don't understand how important it is to your future."

"I think I do," I admitted.

"I've been offered a position in Charlotte for the next school year, which I had planned to take," she went on, "because it's a sure thing, you see. But I will turn it down if you want me to go with you to Chapel Hill. I can always apply to the schools there. If I can't get a job teaching right away, then I'll do whatever I have to do until something opens up for me. I know I can wait on tables. I'm a good waitress."

"Oh, Mama, you would do that for me?"

"I would do anything for you. And who knows? I might even like Chapel Hill. Maybe eventually I can work on my master's degree there."

"And we can live together? I won't have to live in the dorm?" I said.

"That's right. We'll rent an apartment; then later we can buy a house, if all goes well for us."

It seemed like the perfect solution: go to this special magnet school, and still live with Mama. Then why didn't I jump at the chance? Maybe I would.

Still, there was Daddy, Lindy, Grandma and Papa, Bucky, my other relatives and friends, Melba and the twins, Whisper and Sunset, the Wild Girl, the bird sanctuary, the Tarheel, the fish pond, the cemetery . . .

"I'll have to think about it," I said.

"You have until the end of this month to get your application in," she reminded me. "So think fast."

That weekend I discussed it with Daddy. We went for a walk in the woods, and I told him all the things I would miss.

"That's right," Daddy said. "You've never known another place. You'd be giving up a lot."

"But look how much I will be giving up if I don't go," I said.

"What do you think this Wolfe House has to offer you?" he said.

"It's a chance to study poetry. I can be with other creative writers and have the most talented teachers in the field."

"But you will have to leave Buttermilk Hill to do that," Daddy persisted. "This is your home."

And something occurred to me.

"Daddy, is that why you never accepted the offer from the St. Louis Cardinals? Because you didn't want to leave home?"

Our eyes met in that moment, and for the first time in our lives there was perfect understanding between us.

"I will send you extra money," he said.

36

My application to Wolfe House was in before the deadline, and Mama applied to every school in the Chapel Hill areas. In a matter of weeks, her mail was full of requests for interviews. There appeared to be a shortage of music teachers. She was confident that one of the positions would work out for her.

By the end of April I received my acceptance to Wolfe House. So it was settled, and Mama and I celebrated. We planned to leave the day after she graduated from college.

Mama sold the trailer through a newspaper ad, and it was to be moved the day we vacated it. The money from the trailer would help us live through the summer until Mama began teaching.

We packed all of our belongings, except for two suitcases, in boxes, and stored them in Daddy's barn. He agreed to bring them down to us in Chapel Hill as soon as we found a place to live. Now that they would be living a hundred miles apart, he and Mama had decided to be friends. It was nothing close to the reconciliation I had dreamed of, but it was something.

Saying goodbye to Lindy was the hardest part. But we made plans to visit. I would come back for every holiday, and Lindy would visit us often on weekends. Both she and I, and Bucky, too, had decided we wanted to go to college at Chapel Hill.

There were farewell parties and tears and kisses until I was sick of saying goodbye. On our last morning in Buttermilk Hill, Mama and I got up very early, before the town was awake, and escaped before we had to say goodbye again. We loaded ourselves and Booger quickly into June Bug with our luggage, and headed out to the highway.

As we passed the sign that said we were leaving Buttermilk Hill, the sun was just coming up. We looked at each other and smiled with tears in our eyes, knowing in that moment that we were wild beautiful birds leaving the sanctuary, and flying toward the horizon, chasing a dream.

My Home Town
by Piper Berry (age 14)

I am the girl you watched
 Turning cartwheels down a hill
 Of buttermilk daisies and sweet-tasting clover
 On endless summer days and mosquito-biting nights.

I am the fish, the crickets, the frogs in the ponds
   Of Buttermilk Hill
   Who sing out on hot sticky nights the same
   Mournful song, as days become shorter and all
      seasons must turn.

I am the stories spun at the Curl Up and Dye
   Unfolding and falling, unforgettable and full
There for the taking or swept away by day's end.

I am the smell of bread baking, cookies cooking, of
      homemade pickles
   Simmering
   On the back of the stove at the Tarheel Truck Stop
   Sizzling. Brewing. Popping. Stirring. Welcomes
      you in.

I am the voices, resting and peaceful
   That lie under the earth
   Mixing with time and change and forever
Under the shade of the grand aging trees
Under the gentle warmth of the sun
Under the soft and green growing grass
   Speaking of patience and history long gone.
I am all of these things. And more. Much more.

But if someday I have to leave—
If someday I must learn to fly—

I will take my lesson from this sanctuary.
From this hometown sky upon which I glide
From the people who have loved me
And whom I have loved
From the promise of wild flowers growing in
Buttermilk Hill,
And blanketing my world.